She found Jacob standing on her back porch staring at the mountains.

She'd always loved the view and the quiet, but it struck her that she was completely isolated.

A shiver tore through her. Anyone could sneak through the woods and break in through the back door or window.

Jacob turned to look at her, and another shiver rippled through her. This time not from fear. A sensual awareness that she hadn't felt in a long time heated her blood.

Her gaze locked with his, and tension simmered between them.

"You okay?" he asked gruffly.

She nodded, although she wasn't okay. The memory of his arms and solid chest against hers made her crave the safety of his embrace again. But leaning on Jacob could become a habit.

He was being nice only because it was his job. And she needed him to do that and find her daughter more than she needed him to hold her.

MYSTERIOUS ABDUCTION

USA TODAY Bestselling Author

RITA HERRON

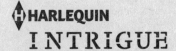

HARLEQUIN

INTRIGUE

To the fans who belong to the Addicted to Danger Loop—hope
you enjoy this new series!

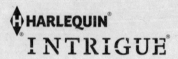

ISBN-13: 978-1-335-13634-3

Mysterious Abduction

Copyright © 2020 by Rita B. Herron

All rights reserved. No part of this book may be used or reproduced in
any manner whatsoever without written permission except in the case of
brief quotations embodied in critical articles and reviews.

This is a work of fiction. Names, characters, places and incidents
are either the product of the author's imagination or are used fictitiously.
Any resemblance to actual persons, living or dead, businesses,
companies, events or locales is entirely coincidental.

This edition published by arrangement with Harlequin Books S.A.

For questions and comments about the quality of this book,
please contact us at CustomerService@Harlequin.com.

Harlequin Enterprises ULC
22 Adelaide St. West, 40th Floor
Toronto, Ontario M5H 4E3, Canada
www.Harlequin.com

Printed in U.S.A.

Recycling programs
for this product may
not exist in your area.

USA TODAY bestselling author **Rita Herron** wrote her first book when she was twelve but didn't think real people grew up to be writers. Now she writes so she doesn't have to get a real job. A former kindergarten teacher and workshop leader, she traded storytelling to kids for writing romance, and now she writes romantic comedies and romantic suspense. Rita lives in Georgia with her family. She loves to hear from readers, so please visit her website, ritaherron.com.

Visit the Author Profile page at Harlequin.com.

CAST OF CHARACTERS

Cora Reeves—She'll do anything to find her missing baby—including trust the sheriff who seems to believe in her.

Sheriff Jacob Maverick—He'll do anything to protect Cora. Even if it means reopening his painful past.

Kurt Philips—The private investigator was murdered investigating the kidnapping of Cora's daughter.

Drew Westbrook—Did Cora's ex have something to do with his baby going missing?

Hilary Westbrook—Does Drew's new wife know who abducted his daughter?

Faye Fuller—She's running from something.

Nina Fuller—Could Faye's adopted daughter be Cora's child?

Prologue

They say that you forget what labor is like the moment you hold your baby in your arms.

Cora Reeves Westbrook would never forget.

Still, her little girl was worth every painful contraction.

Cora leaned back against the pillow in the hospital bed and gently traced a finger over her daughter's soft cheek. Alice smelled like baby shampoo and all things good and sweet in life.

Her husband, Drew, dropped a kiss on her forehead. It had been a rough eighteen hours, and she hadn't slept in almost two days, but she'd never been happier.

Her little girl was perfect.

She memorized every inch of her small round face, her little pug nose, her ten little fingers and toes, and that dimple in her right cheek.

"She's the most beautiful baby I've ever seen," she whispered.

"She looks like an angel," Drew murmured.

Cora smiled, grateful he seemed happy, too. When she'd first told Drew about the pregnancy, he hadn't been thrilled. He was worried about finances and had his goals set on a partnership at his law firm. She'd assured him they could handle a family, but he'd still obsessed over the possibility of not being financially secure.

His cell phone buzzed, and he gave her an apologetic look. "Sorry, I need to get this."

He hurried from the room, and she pressed a kiss to Alice's cheek and rocked her back and forth, whispering promises of love.

A few minutes later, Lisa, the nurse who'd helped her during delivery, appeared again.

"We need to take her to run some tests." She patted Cora's leg. "I'll bring her back in a bit. You should rest. Those night feedings can wear you out."

Cora hugged Alice one more time, then handed her to the nurse. She was so excited that she didn't think she could sleep, but exhaustion overcame her the minute the nurse left the room, and she drifted off.

She was dreaming of carrying Alice home to the nursery she'd decorated when the scent of smoke woke her. Suddenly the fire alarm sounded, and the door burst open. Lisa raced in.

"Come on, we have to evacuate!"

She raced to the bed to help Cora, but panic sent Cora flying off the bed first. "My baby! I have to get Alice!"

"The neonatal nurses are already moving the infants outside," Lisa said. "We'll find her out there!"

Cora pushed the nurse aside and ran into the hall. Thick smoke fogged her vision, chaos erupting around her. The staff was hurrying to help patients out, pushing wheelchairs and beds, and assisting those who needed help. Someone grabbed her arm.

"Go down the stairs!"

"My baby!" Cora pushed at the hands, stumbled and

felt her way to the window of the nursery. Screams and cries echoed around her as firefighters raced into the hall.

She pressed her face to the glass partition and peered inside, searching for her baby.

But the room was empty.

A sob caught in her throat. Her mind raced. *Outside.* The nurse said they were moving the infants outside.

She tore away from the window and stumbled toward the stairs. The hall was full now, patients and staff frantic to reach the exits. Someone pushed her forward, and she was carried into the stairwell. She clawed at the railing to stay on her feet as she raced down the stairs.

When they reached the landing, someone opened the door to the bottom floor, but heat blasted her. Flames were ripping through the hall. A terrified scream echoed in her ears. Another patient's—or her own? She didn't know. Maybe both.

A fireman appeared and pointed toward a back exit. She covered her mouth, coughing as smoke filled her lungs, then followed as everyone crouched low to make it outside.

Lights from the fire truck and police twirled in the sky. Beds, wheelchairs filled with the injured and those too weak to walk, patients, family, visitors and hospital workers poured onto the lawn. Doctors, nurses and medics were circulating to tend to the hurt and sick. Flames shot from the building and firefighters scurried to douse the blaze. First responders rushed inside to save lives.

A coughing fit seized her, but she brushed aside the medic who approached her. "The babies? Where are they?"

He turned and scanned the area, then pointed to a corner near the parking lot. Cora took off running; she was so weak that her legs wobbled unsteadily. She searched faces for Drew but didn't see him, either.

God, please, let him have Alice.

Praying with all her might, she staggered through the mess, the terrified and pain-filled screams of the injured filling the smoky air. Finally she spotted a row of bassinets.

Tears blurred her eyes, but she stumbled forward and frantically began to search the bassinets. Other parents were doing the same, two nurses trying to organize the chaos and failing as frightened mothers dragged their infants into their arms.

Cora finally spotted the bassinet marked "Westbrook—Girl" and gripped the edge of it.

She reached inside, but her baby was gone.

Chapter One

Five years later

Cora's phone beeped as she let herself into her house, but she was juggling a grocery bag and bottle of Chardonnay and couldn't reach it. She and her ex-husband, Drew, had bought the little bungalow nestled in the mountains of North Carolina six years ago when they'd first married—and were happy.

Before Alice was taken.

That day the world stopped for Cora.

Sometimes she wanted to give up. To die and be rid of the pain.

But every time she reached for the razor blade to slit her wrists, she saw her baby's face in her mind. Sweet, precious Alice with the little round face and a cherub nose and a gummy smile.

A tiny six-pound infant who'd trusted her mother to take care of her.

But Cora had failed.

Her baby was out there somewhere. Cora wasn't going to give up until she found her.

Unlike Drew, who'd abandoned Cora a few months after their baby had disappeared.

Cora wanted to hold Alice and assure her that all she'd ever wanted was to be her mommy. She wanted to rock her when she didn't feel good and clean her boo-boos and pick her up when she fell.

Her phone vibrated again, indicating she had a message. Maybe it was the principal of the elementary school where she taught, saying he'd changed his mind and she hadn't been fired.

When the last bell had rung today, he'd summoned her into his office.

"Cora, I understand how painful losing your daughter was, but you frightened Nina Fuller. Her mother called me to complain."

"I heard she was adopted—"

"I'm well aware of the family's situation, and you overstepped."

"But I thought—"

"You thought about your own obsession," he said, cutting her off. "Not about how that woman had three miscarriages and was on a wait list to adopt for three years before they got Nina."

Cora's heart squeezed. She hadn't known about the miscarriages and was sure the woman had suffered.

"I'm sorry," Cora said sincerely. "I'll apologize to Nina and her mother."

He held up a warning hand. "No, you are to leave them alone. Enough is enough. You need to take a break from teaching and get some help."

He meant psychiatric help. She had already done that. It hadn't worked.

The only thing that would make her whole again was to find her daughter. To tell her how much she loved her. That she'd been looking for her every day since that awful fire when someone had stolen her.

At first she'd been terrified that her baby had died in the fire. But after a massive search of the hospital and grounds, the police found Alice's hospital bracelet tossed on the ground near the parking lot.

That bracelet led them all to believe that someone had abducted Alice during the chaos.

"I promise I'll be more careful—"

"You don't understand, Cora," he said firmly. "This is not a suggestion. I'm terminating your employment."

Panic stabbed at Cora. He wasn't renewing her contract for the fall?

Oh, God, what was she going to do? Teaching had been her salvation the last few years. Her connection with children.

Her way to search for her missing daughter. Every year when the new students piled in, she studied the girls' faces for any detail she'd recognize. Some part of her that her offspring had inherited.

She did the same thing on the street, and at the mall and even the market she'd just left.

She dropped the grocery bag on the counter along with the bottle of wine. Summer break was always difficult as it meant endless hours alone, hours of reliving the past and praying that one day she'd find her little girl. Endless hours of the what-ifs that plagued her and threatened to steal her sanity.

She fished her phone from her purse. Sweat beaded on her forehead when she saw the number for Kurt Philips on the caller ID.

Kurt was the private investigator she'd kept on retainer for the last four years. She'd hired him the day after the police had declared that her case had gone cold.

Drew had left a few months after Alice went missing, and within a year, he'd remarried and started another family. His desertion and the fact that he'd had a son with his new wife had almost broken her.

Maybe Kurt had news.

Too afraid to hope, she uncorked the wine, poured a glass and carried it to the deck off the kitchen. Her backyard overlooked the beautiful mountains and Whistling River, the river the small mountain town of Whistler was named after. A summer breeze ruffled the pines as she sat down on the wrought iron glider and checked her voice mail.

"Cora, it's Kurt." His gruff voice was familiar, but he sounded different. Tense. Worried.

Then he was cut off.

She started to call him back, but a text came through.

Sorry, lead didn't pan out. It's time we give it a rest. You should move on.

His words sent pain searing through Cora. Kurt couldn't give up. He was her last hope.

With a shaky finger, she quickly pressed Call Back. But the phone rang and rang and no one answered.

Desperate to talk to him, she carried her glass of wine back to the kitchen, grabbed her keys and purse and jogged outside to her car.

Kurt had not only worked for her. He'd been her friend the last year.

He'd also cautioned her to prepare for the worst. Had

he learned that something bad had happened to her baby and he didn't want to tell her?

She jumped in her vehicle, started the engine and peeled down her driveway onto the street. She couldn't go on without answers.

She had to know why he was abandoning her and the search for Alice.

SHERIFF JACOB MAVERICK parked in the strip shopping center on the edge of town, grimacing at the flames shooting into the sky. The fire department was already on the scene, rolling out hoses and spraying water to douse the blaze.

His brother Griff, a firefighter and arson investigator, was suited up and heading into the building.

Déjà vu struck Jacob and he froze, fear gripping him. He'd lost his father, the sheriff at the time of the horrific hospital fire that had nearly destroyed the town five years ago.

He couldn't lose one of his brothers.

But he couldn't stop Griff from doing his job any more than his brothers could have stopped him from taking over as sheriff after their father died. They all wanted to know who set that fire. They suspected arson. So far, though, they didn't have answers.

But one day he would find the truth.

His father's heroic behavior had inspired each of his brothers to become first responders. Griff had joined the fire department. Fletch, FEMA's local Search and Rescue team. And Liam, the FBI.

Lights from the ambulance twirled against the darkening sky. His deputy, Martin Rowan, had cordoned off the area to keep people away from the blaze. Jacob climbed from his vehicle and strode toward Martin.

"What do we have?" he asked.

Martin shrugged. "Not sure yet. The guy in the insurance office two doors down called it in. Said he came back for some paperwork and spotted smoke."

"The building looks old," Jacob said. "Could be faulty electrical wiring."

Wood crackled and popped. Flames were eating the downstairs and climbing through the second floor. Thick gray smoke billowed above, pouring out the windows and obliterating the puffy white clouds. Firefighters aimed the hoses and worked to extinguish the blaze.

A crash sounded, glass exploded. The roof...collapsed.

His pulse hammered and he ran toward the front door. The raging heat hit him in the face. "Come on, Griff," he muttered. "Get the hell out."

A CHILL RIPPLED through Cora as she passed Whistler's graveyard on the way to Kurt's office. Many of the people who'd died in the town fire had been buried in that cemetery. She jerked her eyes away, determined not to allow her mind to travel to the dark place it had so many times before.

Kurt's text made that impossible.

Had he found evidence indicating her daughter was...dead?

No...she wouldn't let herself believe that. A mother would know. *She* would know if that was true.

Night was falling, storm clouds shrouding the remaining sunlight. With Whistler so close to the Appalachian Trail, the area drew tourists during the summer months. People flocked to the cooler mountains to escape the heat, to indulge in hiking, camping, fishing and white water rafting.

When Alice was first taken, Cora had been shocked at how people laughed and went on about life when she could barely breathe for the anguish.

Tonight the breeze blowing off the water sounded shrill and eerie, a reminder that danger also existed in the endless miles of thick forests and the class four rapids. It also brought the scent of smoke.

She glanced to the right in the direction of Kurt's office, and her pulse jumped. Thick plumes of gray smoke were rolling upward.

She pressed the accelerator and swerved around an SUV, then wove past a caravan of church groups in white vans with the sign Jesus Saves emblazoned on the sides. She swung to the right onto a side street and bounced over a rut in the country road. A mile from the main highway, she reached the strip shopping center. Lights from fire trucks and emergency vehicles swirled against the darkness.

She veered into the shopping center, her gaze tracking the chaos. Flames had engulfed one building and lit the sky.

Dear God. It was Kurt's building.

She threw the car into Park on the hill near the tattoo parlor. Fear clawed at her.

Seconds ticked by. Other rubberneckers had gathered to watch the commotion.

Police worked to secure the area and keep onlookers away. A minute later, a firefighter raced out, carrying a man over his shoulder.

She craned her neck to see but couldn't tell if it was

Kurt. Then she spotted a pair of boots. Gray and black. Snakeskin. Silver spurs.

Kurt's boots.

Boots she recognized because she'd given them to him.

Chapter Two

Jacob jogged toward Griff as his brother eased the man onto the stretcher by the ambulance. Instant recognition hit Jacob. "This is Kurt Philips, a private investigator. He was working for Cora. He talked to me about her case a few times."

Griff removed his oxygen mask and helmet, then shook his head. "He was dead when I found him." He gestured toward the bloody mess that had been the man's chest. He'd been shot.

The stench of burnt flesh, charred skin and ash swirled around Jacob. Damn. The fire was most likely arson intended to cover up a murder.

Considering the fact that Philips was a PI, he could have been killed because of one of his cases. His files, which might hold the answer to his killer's identity, had probably been destroyed in the blaze. Could have been the killer's intent.

The ME, a doctor named Ryland Hammerhead, bent over the corpse on the stretcher to examine the body.

"Got an ID?" Dr. Hammerhead asked.

Jacob nodded. "Kurt Philips, private investigator." Which opened up a lot of possibilities for who would want him dead.

The ME photographed the corpse, then brushed soot from his shirt. "COD is probably blood loss from the gunshot wound to the chest, but I'll conduct a thorough autopsy and update you when I finish."

"Once the fire dies down, I'll have a crime team search the debris for evidence," Jacob said.

"I'll dig out the bullet and send it to the lab." The ME lifted Philips's right hand to examine it. Even through the dirt and ash, Jacob spotted blood. Dr. Hammerhead cut open the man's shirt, and Jacob zeroed in on the gunshot wound. The bullet hole had ripped skin and muscle and shattered bone.

He snapped a close-up with his cell phone.

"Must have been shot at close range." Jacob relayed the scene in his head. "Victim raised his hand to stop the bullet."

Dr. Hammerhead nodded grimly. "And was too late."

"Call me when you're ready with your report," Jacob said. "I'll meet you at the morgue."

The doctor gestured to the medics to load the body for transporting. Jacob joined his deputy and filled him in. He scrutinized the curious onlookers who'd gathered. "Canvass the crowd and store owners and find out if anyone saw anything. A car leaving, maybe?"

Martin nodded. "I'll get right on it."

Jacob scanned the parking lot. Sometimes thrill-seeking perps stuck around to watch the chaos and fear created by their crime. A vehicle on the crest of the hill in the parking lot caught his eye. Firelight illuminated the sky, making it easy to see the car. A red Ford SUV.

Cora Reeves's SUV.

Damn. His heart ached for that woman. Everyone in town knew about the baby she'd lost during the fire—

the baby she believed had been kidnapped. He'd worked the case afterward and been frustrated as hell when the case went cold.

Was Philips murdered because he'd found out something about her child?

NERVES BUNCHED IN Cora's stomach. If the sheriff learned about the message Kurt had left her, he'd want to talk to her.

She'd seen enough of the press and police in her lifetime. They hadn't done a bit of good when her baby disappeared. Sure, Jacob, who'd been the deputy back then, had tried to find Alice, but he'd also been grief-stricken over his father's death. The entire town had been in shock and suffering from their personal losses, and confusion came from the chaos and terror. The massive extent of the damage from the blaze had also complicated evidence recovery.

Jacob had even questioned her as if she was a suspect. As if she'd paid someone to take her infant off her hands.

Then police focused on Drew. The questions and interrogations had compounded the agony and destroyed their marriage. Or maybe it had been her obsession with finding her daughter...

Emotions welling in her throat, Cora started the engine and drove away from the scene. But as the flames flickered behind her, lighting up the sky, despair overwhelmed her.

If Kurt was dead, she was really, truly alone.

And her chances of learning what happened to her daughter had died with him.

The rest of the drive blurred as a storm threatened.

By the time she reached the house, her hands ached from clenching the steering wheel. She pulled into the garage, closed the electric door and rushed inside. The wine she'd poured earlier was still sitting on the kitchen counter, a reminder that she'd lost her job earlier that day. That summer loomed with the threat of her bank account dwindling.

She curled her fingers around the stem of the wine-glass and climbed the stairs to the second floor. To the nursery she'd decorated for Alice.

Tears clogged her throat as she stepped inside. The pale pink color of the walls still remained. But the furniture and baby clothes had all been removed.

Drew had packed them up one day while she was at her therapist's office. He'd said he couldn't stand to see her stare at the baby toys and clothes, so he'd given them away. He wanted them to move on.

Move on as if they'd never had a child? Erase any evidence she'd given birth.

She'd told him to get out. He might be able to forget about their daughter. But she would never forget.

Exhausted, she decided to shower. Maybe the running water would wash away the images of Kurt being carried from that burning building. She scrubbed her hands and body, then her hair, and let the tears fall. Tears for Kurt.

Tears for the loneliness and emptiness she felt.

Tears of fear that Kurt's death meant she'd never find Alice.

The doorbell rang, startling her, and she stepped from the shower and dried off. She pulled on her bath-robe and ran a comb through her damp hair.

The doorbell rang again. Who would be visiting her

this time of night? She'd lost most of her friends over the years.

Nerves on edge, she hurried to the window and looked outside. The sheriff's car sat in her drive.

JACOB STOOD ON Cora's front porch, tapping his boot as he waited for her to answer the door. He'd left his deputy to guard the crime scene and would go back once the blaze died down and it was safe for the crime scene team to search for forensics. Griff would look for the origin of the fire and traces of accelerant.

Maybe the killer had been sloppy, hadn't used gloves and had left a print. Doubtful, although if the perp thought the fire would completely destroy evidence, he might not have been so careful.

He rang the bell again.

Finally footsteps echoed from the inside. He braced himself to see Cora in person again. She'd come to his office at least once a month over the years to see if he had news. The pain in her eyes always tore him inside out. He'd lost a father, but he couldn't imagine losing a child. Living with unanswered questions, wondering if she was dead or alive. Safe or happy. If she had a home...

He'd heard rumors that Cora had become so obsessed with finding her daughter that she'd pushed friends away. Her marriage had fallen apart, too. Her bastard husband had walked out a few months after the baby disappeared, then remarried, and Cora had reclaimed her maiden name.

He'd never trusted her ex. Drew Westbrook had been at the top of his suspect list five years ago. Jacob just hadn't been able to prove that he'd been involved in his baby's disappearance.

Maybe Kurt had found a lead.

He inhaled a deep breath at the sound of the door lock turning. The moment he saw Cora's tear-swollen eyes, though, he knew Kurt Philips hadn't given her good news.

"Hi, Cora. Can I come in?"

Her deep, sad blue eyes pierced him, as if she hadn't forgotten that he'd let her down. Guilt gnawed at him. He had tried. But he'd failed.

She clutched her robe around her and cinched the belt. Jacob's lungs squeezed for air. Even sad and wearing that cotton bathrobe, Cora looked sexy with her damp, long, wavy auburn hair brushing her shoulders.

A wary look darkened her face, but she stepped aside and gestured for him to come in. He wiped his feet on the welcome mat in the entry, noting that she hadn't changed anything since he'd been here before. The decor was still the same—tasteful but simple.

The open concept living/dining kitchen was furnished in what he thought they called farmhouse style. A distressed-looking table and chairs sat to the left in front of the front window while a large island divided the living room and kitchen. A floor-to-ceiling brick fireplace made the room look cozy, although he'd wondered more than once why Cora hadn't moved from town to escape the painful memories.

Maybe she thought whoever took her baby might bring her to Whistler?

Cora led him to the kitchen and offered him coffee. She had one of those new coffee makers that made a cup at a time using pods, and fixed him a cup. He had a feeling she was stalling, because she knew why he was here.

He accepted a mug of coffee, and waited as she made herself one. Then she led him to the den. She sank onto the couch, and he claimed the leather wing chair by the fireplace.

"I saw you at Kurt Philips's office tonight. The place burned down."

She looked down into her mug. "Do you know what started the fire?"

He shook his head. "Not yet. We'll be conducting a thorough investigation."

She lifted her gaze, her blue eyes piercing him again. "Shouldn't you be there now doing that?"

The disapproval in her tone made him grit his teeth. "I'll go back once the fire dies down and the investigators can get in." He took a sip of his coffee. "I know Kurt Philips was a PI, Cora, and that he worked for you." He intentionally let the statement linger. Not a question really, but he wanted to see her reaction.

She shifted and tucked her feet underneath her on the sofa as if she was relaxed. But tension oozed from her stiff posture and the tight set of her slender jaw.

Cora was an attractive woman, naturally pretty, wholesome and kindhearted. She did volunteer work with the church to pack meals for needy families.

"He did," Cora admitted.

"I'm sorry, Cora. You probably think I gave up, but I haven't. Liam has kept your case high on the FBI's priority list." Griff continued to search for arson cases similar to the hospital fire in hopes of making a connection. Fletch was keeping an eye out on his search and rescue missions in case the arsonist—killer—was holed up in the woods off the grid.

Her eyes widened as if surprised. "Liam really is looking for Alice?"

Jacob nodded. "I swear, Cora. One day we'll find her."

Emotions streaked her face, and she closed her eyes for a brief moment, pinching the bridge of her nose. When she opened her eyes again, she blinked away tears.

"Did Kurt have any leads for you?" Jacob asked.

She dropped her gaze to her coffee again. "No. He hadn't found anything yet."

Jacob heard the disappointment in her tone. "When did you last see or speak to him?"

She shifted again, and Jacob had the impression she was hiding something.

"Come on, Cora, talk to me," Jacob said. "I need to know what happened at his office."

"I don't know," she said. "Maybe it was an accidental fire?"

He shook his head. "Listen to me," he said gruffly. "The fire was set to cover up something else."

"You mean a theft? Did someone rob his office?"

"I don't know yet, but that's possible," he admitted. "But it was more than a robbery."

"What do you mean?"

"Kurt Philips was murdered."

Chapter Three

Cora gripped her coffee mug so hard she thought it would shatter. "What?" she said in a raw whisper.

A muscle ticked in Jacob's jaw. "I'm sorry, Cora, but Kurt was murdered."

"How? Why?"

His gaze locked with hers. Jacob had always been intimidating. Big, muscular, strong, with a wide, chiseled jaw and dark brown eyes that seemed as if they could see into her soul. She felt as if he was looking there now.

Probing. Wondering. Just like the other cops and FBI had. He couldn't possibly think she'd killed Kurt, could he?

"Just tell me when you talked to him or saw him last?"

The fact that he ignored her question raised her defensive instincts. She could not go here again, not be treated like a suspect.

"I don't remember," she said, hedging. "He works cases other than mine. Do you think he was killed because of one of those?"

Silence stretched between them for a tension-filled minute. "It's too early to tell. But I'll examine all his cases. Although the murder could have been personal. Was he married or involved with anyone?"

She fought a reaction. "I don't know, *Sheriff*." She intentionally emphasized his title. "Now, is that all?"

His gaze latched with hers. Again, his look was so probing that she almost squirmed.

"I thought he might have uncovered something about your daughter." He shrugged, but his demeanor didn't quite meet the nonjudgmental attitude he was trying to convey. "If one of his cases got him killed, Cora, it might have been yours."

Her breath caught. Was he right?

Had Kurt discovered who'd taken Alice and been killed so he'd be quiet?

If so, why had he texted that he was giving up?

JACOB SENSED CORA was holding something back. She looked visibly shaken by the news that Philips was dead. Even more so that he might have been killed because he was looking for Alice.

Or perhaps she was just upset that she'd lost her PI. God knew she'd suffered a lot of knocks over the past five years with her daughter's case going cold and then her divorce. Every day it ate at him that they didn't know who'd set that fire at the hospital, because that person had killed his father, taken more lives and possibly kidnapped Cora's daughter.

She lived with that pain every day, as well, wondering where her little girl was and what had happened to her.

He glanced at her hands. She'd obviously just showered before he'd arrived, so if she had shot Kurt, she'd washed away gunshot residue. He had no probable cause at this point to even test her for it.

Besides, he didn't see Cora as a killer. She was soft, vulnerable and compassionate. She taught school at Whistler Elementary.

"You aren't certain that Kurt was killed because he worked for me, though, are you?" Cora asked.

Jacob shook his head. "Not at this point. We need to search his files and records of his other cases, although the fire is going to complicate that. I'm not sure how much we can salvage." He studied her. "Did he talk to you about anything else he was working on?"

She shook her head no.

"What about his personal life? Did he have family? A wife?"

She shifted and sipped her coffee. "He had no family that I know of. And he was divorced."

He'd talk to the ex. "How long ago was that?"

"A few months, I think." She wrinkled her nose in thought. "He didn't share the details."

"Do you know his ex-wife's name or where she lives?"

She stood and ran a hand through her still-damp hair. She was trembling. From the shock of the news or something else? "I think her name was Erica. He mentioned her once when he asked me about Drew. I have no idea where she lives."

"You two never met?"

"No." She folded her arms.

"Was the divorce amicable?"

"Like I said, he didn't share details, although I had the impression she wanted him back."

If that was the case and Kurt had been dating someone else, his ex might have been jealous and killed him because he rejected her.

Definitely an avenue to explore.

"Thanks for seeing me, Cora," Jacob said. "If you think of anything else that might be helpful, please call me."

She nodded but seemed reluctant as she walked him to the door.

"Jacob?"

Her soft voice, so full of need, made his chest clench. He leaned against the door and faced her. Maybe she had been holding back and was ready to come clean. "Yes?"

"Did you mean what you said about your brother looking for Alice?"

The inkling of hope in her tone stirred his protective instincts. "Yes. It's difficult without current photographs to distribute, but he's kept her file active. He also has someone looking at adoptions that occurred around that time."

She sucked in a deep breath. "If it would help, I've drawn sketches projecting what Alice might look like at every age. I based them on photos of me and of Drew when we were young."

He didn't know what to say.

"I guess that sounds crazy," she said in a haunted whisper. "But I like to draw."

Jacob heard the ache in her words and shook his head. "You don't sound crazy. And it might be helpful if you sent me some of those drawings. I'll pass them to Liam, and he can distribute to other law enforcement agencies and NCEMC. We might get lucky and someone will recognize her."

Hope lit her eyes. God help him, he didn't want to

let her down again. He understood the disappointment when a clue didn't pan out.

He'd chased dead leads in search of his father's killer since that damn fire.

But at least he knew where his father was. He had closure.

Cora lived with uncertainty every day.

Cora cleared her throat. "I can drop some sketches by your office tomorrow if that's all right."

He nodded. "That works."

"One more question, Cora. Did Kurt question Drew?"

She hesitated. "Yes, along with everyone who was at the hospital at the time."

"How did it go with Drew?"

"Not well," she admitted.

He didn't expect it had. Drew had been furious when Jacob questioned him. He'd set his sights on making partner at his law firm, and had threatened to sue the sheriff's office if they maligned his character with accusations.

Ironically, the publicity had catapulted him into the limelight and earned him sympathy from his coworkers. He'd made partner a few months after the kidnapping.

Then he'd left Cora to deal with the emotional fallout of looking for their child alone.

Drew wouldn't like to be questioned again. But Jacob wouldn't allow Drew's attitude to deter him.

If the bastard had anything to do with the PI's death, Jacob would find out.

JACOB'S WORDS ECHOED in Cora's ears. *We might get lucky and someone will recognize her.*

He'd said *we,* as if she wasn't alone. As if he truly hadn't given up. As if there might be a chance to find her daughter...

Heart hammering, she hurried up the steps to the room that had been meant for her baby. In her mind, she pictured it filled with all the precious things she'd received at her baby shower—the giant teddy bear and sweet little embroidered dresses. The tiny white kids' table and the storybooks. The pink-and-white polka-dotted sheets and the dancing bear mobile she'd hung over the white Jenny Lind crib.

The memory of the day she'd come home from therapy and found the room empty taunted her.

Drew had been standing at the empty nursery, stoic and calm. "The therapist suggested it might help you move on if we cleaned out the baby's room."

Seeing that empty room had nearly brought her to her knees. "I don't want to move on!" she'd screamed. "I want to find my daughter. I thought you did, too."

Pain wrenched his face. "I do, Cora. But... I can't go on like this. Day after day listening to you cry. Watching you touch the baby clothes and sleep with her stuffed animals. You're driving yourself crazy."

"You mean I'm driving you crazy," she shouted.

"Yes. I'm trying to hold it together, but I can't do it anymore. I can't hold us both together."

"What are you saying? That you're giving up on finding Alice?"

"I'm not giving up," he said, "but it's been months. The leads have gone cold. Bills are piling up. My boss is pressuring me to see clients again. I have to resume my practice or I'll never make partner. It might do you good to return to teaching."

"My life *is* my daughter." She'd waved her hand across the room. "Where are her things? I want them back."

"I took them to a shelter," he said in a low, tired voice. "People need them, Cora. We don't."

"Alice will need them when she comes home."

His eyes narrowed to slits, then a tear slid down his cheek. "What if she doesn't come home? We have to face that possibility—"

"No!" She lunged at him. "You can't give up and forget about her!"

He stood ramrod straight while she hit him in the chest with her fists and cried. Finally she spent her emotions and sagged against him. Then he pushed her away and walked out the door.

Cora fought despair. The moment the door slammed, she'd known her marriage was over. That losing Alice had torn them apart.

She crossed the room to the hope chest she'd bought after Drew moved out. Inside it, she'd placed cards, letters and gifts for every birthday and holiday that had passed. Stuffed animals, baby dolls and puzzles. Books and crayons and coloring books. A pumpkin Halloween costume and a red Christmas dress. Soft ballerina shoes and bows for Alice's hair.

The wrapping paper was fading now, ribbons crushed. But she'd kept them so if—no, *when*—she found Alice, she'd prove that she'd never forgotten her.

The only thing Drew hadn't given away was the pink-and-green blanket she'd crocheted before Alice was born.

She removed the blanket from the chest and pressed it to her face, the yarn baby soft.

She'd never gotten to wrap her daughter in that blanket.

The memory of cradling her newborn in her arms was so distant that she felt as if she was clawing at thin air to grasp it, but just as her fingertips reached it, the wind viciously snatched it away.

Tears blurred her eyes, and she moved to the shelf where she kept the journals of her sketches. She'd drawn at least one sketch a week, marking off the days as she tried to imagine the changes in her daughter's face and how she was growing.

She retrieved the latest journal—Alice at five—and studied the sketches. She'd take them all to Jacob tomorrow and let him decide which ones to use.

Although her chest tightened with anxiety. She'd been searching the face of every child she'd seen or met for five years.

Would she even recognize her daughter if she came face-to-face with her?

KNOWING IT WOULD take time for Griff and the crime investigators to comb the scene for forensics, Jacob found the address for Kurt's ex-wife. If Philips had family, she would know. She also needed to be notified of her ex's death.

He wanted to study her reaction when he told her, learn if she had motive for murder.

He phoned his deputy to inform him of his plan. "Make sure Griff and the crime techs recover Philips's cell phone and computer. They could contain information about what he was working on. Any files they can salvage may be valuable."

"On it," Deputy Rowan said.

"I'm headed to Philips's ex-wife's house now. Will keep you posted."

Jacob kept replaying his conversation with Cora in his head as he drove from town. Her anguish was a palpable force.

The last thing he wanted to do was give her false hope.

The clouds darkened in intensity as he veered onto the mountain road leading to Mrs. Philips's house. Trees swayed in the wind as the storm threatened, thunder booming in the distance.

He hoped to hell the rain held off until Griff and the crime team finished. Rain would wash away evidence that was already difficult enough to recover from the ashes and debris of the crumpled building.

His GPS directed him to a side road on the mountain. He maneuvered the turn, slowing as another car barreled around the curve too fast. He let it go by, then steered his SUV up the incline into a small neighborhood built overlooking the mountain.

When he reached the Philipses' house, he turned into the drive and parked. Lights illuminated the inside of the A-frame cabin. He climbed out and strode up to the steps to the front stoop. A black Lab raced over to him, and he paused for a minute to let the dog sniff him. The Lab licked his hand, and Jacob smiled. If Philips's ex had this dog as a watchdog, it was falling down on the job.

He glanced around the property, then knocked. A noise echoed from inside, then footsteps and the door opened. A woman with short, choppy black hair answered, a cocktail in her hand.

"Mrs. Philips?"

She took in his shield and frowned. "Yeah."

"I'm Sheriff Maverick." He took a quick sniff to determine if she smelled of smoke from the fire and detected the scent of cigarette smoke. Hmm…a cigarette lighter could have been used to set the fire. "May I come in?"

She tugged at her T-shirt. "What's this about, Sheriff?"

"We need to talk."

She frowned, but stepped aside and allowed him to enter. The ice in her drink clinked as she took a big swallow. He followed her through a small entryway into her den. Laundry seemed to be spread everywhere, magazines and dirty dishes scattered around.

She plopped down into a big club chair and looked up at him with questions in her eyes. Although her drinking might be a result of knowing her husband was dead—or that she'd murdered him and feared being caught.

But judging from two other empty bottles in the kitchen, Jacob surmised she might have a habit.

"Mrs. Philips, when did you last speak to or see your husband?" he asked.

She crossed her legs, then snagged a pack of cigarettes from the coffee table, tapped one out and lit it. "Last week, I guess."

"Last week? Can you be specific?"

She shrugged. "Maybe Friday. No, wait, it was Saturday."

"You two were separated?"

"Divorced," she said in a tone laced with bitterness. "Eight months ago. Why are you asking about Kurt and me?"

Jacob ignored her question. "Were you and your husband working toward a reconciliation?"

"I wanted it, but Kurt…he was interested in greener pastures." She leaned forward with her hands on her knees, her expression worried. "You sure are asking a lot of questions. Did something happen to Kurt?"

Jacob forced a neutral expression. "Yes, ma'am. I'm sorry to inform you, but he was killed earlier tonight."

Her face paled, and she collapsed back against the sofa, her hand shaking as she raised the cigarette to her lips.

"That's why you asked about our divorce."

He nodded. "I need to know if Kurt had enemies. Or if he was involved with someone else."

Her mouth tightened. "You want to know about Kurt, go ask his girlfriend."

Jacob narrowed his eyes. "Can you give me a name?"

She tapped ashes into an empty soda can on the table. "That lady whose child was kidnapped. She's crazy if you ask me, but Kurt had a thing for her."

Jacob's pulse jumped. "You mean Cora Reeves?"

"That's right." She grabbed her drink and tossed the rest of it down. "I think she was just using him, but he didn't care. Kurt was a sucker for a sob story and that lady had one."

Of course she was using him. She'd hired him to do a job, find her missing daughter. But this woman was implying that Cora and Kurt had a personal relationship.

Was Cora romantically involved with Kurt Philips? If so, why hadn't she told him about it when he'd asked?

Chapter Four

Jacob couldn't get Cora off his mind as he drove home. Were Cora and Kurt personally involved?

He didn't know why the thought bothered him. Cora certainly had suffered when her baby was stolen and her husband deserted her. She deserved to find love again and happiness.

If she had been with Kurt, his death would be another loss.

His chest clenched. The sorrow in her eyes always wrenched his gut.

He parked in the driveway to his cabin on the side of the mountain overlooking the river. Although summer was starting and the temperature was climbing, the air felt cooler and fresher here on the mountain.

Still, the scent of charred wood and metal clung to his skin, a reminder of the fire that had robbed his father's life.

His father's face taunted him as he let himself inside his cabin.

Jacob had always looked up to his old man. Seth Maverick was honest, had fought for justice and worked hard to protect the people in town. All Jacob ever wanted was to be like him.

Six months before the fire, his dream had come true. While other classmates had left the small town, he'd learned to love it the way his father had. He'd attended the police academy, then come home, and his father had deputized him. They'd been doing routine rounds when the 911 call came in about the fire.

Perspiration broke out on the back of Jacob's neck, and he walked through the cabin to the back door, opened it and stepped outside onto the deck that over-looked the canyon and river. A slight breeze stirred the trees, bringing the scent of wildflowers and rain from the day before, yet he was still sweating as the memories bombarded him.

By the time he and his father arrived at the hospital, flames were shooting from one side of the building. The fire alarm had been tripped, and the hospital staff was busy helping patients outside. One fire engine was on the scene and another careened into the parking lot, tires squealing. Emergency workers and firefighters raced to save lives, and roll out hoses to extinguish the blaze.

His father threw the police car into Park, and they both had jumped out to run toward the building. Two firefighters rushed out carrying patients while doctors and nurses and medics combed the lawn to help.

Screams from inside the building had filled the night, part of the roof had collapsed and a window had burst, spraying glass. Smoke poured upward into the night sky.

More firefighters had rushed inside and the volunteer fire department had arrived and jumped into motion to help.

His father didn't hesitate. He had dashed toward the burning building.

Adrenaline surging through him, Jacob had done the same.

For the next half hour, they'd helped people evacuate. Jacob carried more than one ill patient in his arms and pushed wheelchair patients unable to walk on their own.

Another half hour, and the terrified cries and screams were embedded in his memory forever. Family members wove through the crowd on the lawn, searching for loved ones. A man ran from the building, shouting as flames shot from his clothing.

Jacob had rushed toward him, taken his arm and forced him to drop to the ground and roll to extinguish the flames. A medic had jogged toward them and taken over as Jacob hurried to help a pregnant woman down the steps.

Jacob recalled the ear-piercing scream that had suddenly rent the air. Shooting to the source, his gaze found a young woman in a hospital gown by a row of bassinets.

"My baby, my baby!" she cried.

Jacob had sprinted through the crowd to reach her. She was frantic, yelling at one of the nurses.

Tears of fear poured down the woman's face. "My baby…where is she?"

Jacob's lungs strained for air as he realized the bassinet was empty.

"The babies were all here," the nurse said. "We brought them out in the bassinets."

Jacob gripped the woman's arms as a sob tore from her gut. "We'll find her," he murmured. "We'll find her."

Jacob closed his eyes, trying to banish the images after that. The frantic search of the hospital and property for the missing infant. When Drew had finally joined Cora, he'd looked frightened that his daughter wasn't with his wife.

A few minutes later, a staff member ran toward them holding a hospital bracelet he'd found in the parking lot. A hospital bracelet with the name "Baby Westbrook—Girl" on it.

The bracelet that had belonged to Cora's baby.

"We'll find her," he'd promised.

But he hadn't.

He hadn't given up, though. He never would.

EXHAUSTION TUGGED AT Cora the next morning. She stumbled into the kitchen for coffee, made herself a cup and carried it to her screened porch. Dawn was just breaking, the sun streaking the sky in orange, yellow and red. As a teenager, she used to sleep half the morning, but since Alice had been gone, she struggled with insomnia. When she finally slept, nightmares plagued her, and she often rose with the sun.

She loved the peace and quiet of the mountains. The beauty of nature and the rolling hills and the blossoms on the trees.

But once again that peace had been disturbed.

She'd cried herself to sleep over Kurt the night before. He had been a good man. Had been kind to her. Had tried to help her.

She'd let him get closer to her than anyone had in years.

Still, she hadn't totally given him her heart.

That heart had been shattered by the loss of her daughter and her husband and would never be whole again.

Kurt's text still disturbed her.

She heaved a weary breath. Now what?

Jacob…he'd assured her that the FBI hadn't given up on finding her daughter. She'd promised to drop off sketches for his brother to distribute.

She set her coffee aside, rose and went to retrieve the ones she'd pulled the night before. She traced a finger lovingly over each drawing, her heart swelling with love as she imagined finally pulling her daughter into her arms for a hug.

Although her therapist's voice haunted her. *What will you do if you find her and she's in a happy home? Will you upset her world by telling her that you're her mother?*

How could she not tell her if she found her? Her daughter deserved to know that her mother hadn't given her away, didn't she?

She placed the sketches in her tote bag, then checked the clock. Too early to go to the sheriff's office, so she made herself another cup of coffee and took her stationery back to the porch. She settled on the glider and began to write another letter to add to her collection.

Dear Alice,

Today is the first day of summer break. The kids I taught were so excited yesterday. They drew pictures depicting their plans for the break. Some were going swimming. Others are taking vacations to the beach. One little girl is going to Africa with her parents.

I wonder what you're doing this summer. Are you excited that school is out? Or will you miss your friends?

She paused to wipe at a tear, her heart aching. She didn't know one thing about her daughter or her life now. *Did* Alice have friends at school? Did she like music or gymnastics? Was she learning to ride a bicycle? Did she have a pet?

Did she live with two parents who loved her?

Cora swallowed hard and put her pen back to paper again.

I know you're five now and that this year you were in kindergarten. I wonder if you like arts and crafts or sports, and if you're learning to read. One day when I see you again, you can tell me everything.

I still live in the house in the mountains. The flowers are starting to bloom and the wind is whistling off the river this morning. It reminds me of a lullaby I sang to you before you were born. Of all the lullabies I wanted to sing to you when I brought you home.

You're too old for lullabies now. But maybe you like to sing songs you learned at school.

I'm sitting on my back-screened porch thinking about what we would do today if you were here. There's a park close by with a swing set and jungle gym. That would be a fun way to start the day.

We might even take a picnic lunch. Then we can go and get ice cream. There's a cute little ice cream parlor in town called Sundae Heaven, where you can make your own ice cream sundaes. I like vanilla ice cream with hot fudge sauce or fresh strawberries. And my favorite ice cream flavor they have is peach cobbler. It's so yummy!

*I wonder what your favorite flavor is or what
toppings you'd choose. Do you like sprinkles or
chocolate sauce or chocolate chip cookies?*

*I'll tell you a secret. I would love to try Reese's
Peanut Butter Cup ice cream, but I'm allergic to
peanuts! Yikes, I hate those shots!*

*I'll keep you close to my heart until I see you
again.*
All my love,
Mommy

The clock struck the hour, and Cora decided it was
time to shower and take the sketches to Jacob. The
sooner his brother got them into the database, the sooner
someone might recognize Alice.

JACOB'S PHONE WAS ringing as soon as he stepped from
the shower. He dried off, yanked on his clothes and
hurried to answer it.

It was his brother Griff. "I thought you'd want to
know what we found last night."

Jacob walked to the kitchen, poured himself some
coffee and nuked a frozen sausage biscuit. "Yeah, I do."

"The fire was definitely arson. The accelerant—
gasoline. Point of origin, the man's office. I found
traces of gasoline there. Once it was lit, the fire spread
quickly."

No surprise. "Any cigarette butts, matches or a
lighter in the office?"

"No, why?"

"Philips's ex is a smoker." Jacob hesitated. "How
about prints or other forensics?"

"Still working on that," Griff said. "But we did recover a cell phone. I sent it to the lab and just talked to the analyst." He cleared his throat. "The man's last phone call was to Cora Reeves. Looks like it didn't go through. Then he sent a text."

Jacob gritted his teeth. Cora hadn't mentioned a phone call or a text. "What did it say?"

"He said the lead didn't pan out. He was giving up her case."

Jacob's hand tightened around his phone. Cora probably hadn't taken that news well. "Anything else?"

"That's it. Do you think it's important?"

"I don't know yet," Jacob said. "But I'll talk to Cora." He didn't tell his brother that he had already questioned her, and she'd omitted details about her relationship with the man. "Keep me posted."

His brother agreed and hung up. Jacob poured his coffee into a to-go mug, snatched his breakfast sandwich and carried it to his car. Ten minutes later, he was in his office reviewing the original files for the missing Westbrook baby case.

He'd been young and green at detective work at the time. And he'd been grieving for his father. Worse, there were so many people traumatized in the fire. Three lives, other than his father's, had been lost. Several more people had been injured.

He'd enlisted county resources to interview all the parties involved, which had been a nightmare. More than one person in that hospital had enemies.

Whether or not they were strong enough enemies to commit murder had been the question. If targeting a single person, the perp had also endangered hundreds of lives and was now wanted for homicide.

That person had to answer for all the people he'd hurt and the lives he'd destroyed.

He skimmed notes from the deputies who'd assisted in the interviews.

Drew Westbook claimed he'd only stepped out of Cora's hospital room for a few minutes, then the fire alarm had sounded. He'd tried to reach her and the baby, but the firefighters ordered him and everyone else to evacuate via the back stairs.

He'd rushed into the chaos on the lawn. A few minutes later, he'd heard Cora's scream and run to her.

Jacob had to question Westbrook about Kurt Philips.

But first, he'd talk to Cora. She was supposed to drop by with those sketches this morning.

He had to know why she'd lied to him about her relationship with Philips and omitted to tell him about Kurt's text.

CORA WOVE AROUND the curvy mountain road from her house toward town, her nerves on edge.

The phone had rung as she'd dressed, but the caller had hung up. Twice. When she stepped outside, she thought someone had driven by her house and slowed as if looking for her. But when she'd started down her porch steps, the car sped off.

She shivered and maneuvered the switchback, hugging the side of the road as a beige Pontiac car sped toward her. Some people drove way too fast on the mountain road. The narrow switchbacks were the downside to living on the mountain.

Dark storm clouds rolled across the sky, shrouding out the morning sunlight, shadows from the tree limbs dancing across the asphalt. She inhaled and forced her eyes on the road.

Seconds later, the sound of a car engine roared up behind her. She glanced in her rearview mirror as a dark sedan closed in on her tail. Rattled, she steered around the curve hoping he'd slow, but instead the car sped up. She tapped the brakes, urging him to back off. He slowed slightly but sped up again, then rode her rear bumper.

Her heart hammered. Her hands began to sweat. She veered into a driveway leading to some new cabins being built. Finally the car raced by.

God. She must be paranoid. For a moment, she'd thought the car was going to run her off the road.

Breathing out, she dropped her head forward to calm herself. Last night Kurt had been murdered.

Was someone out to kill her, too?

Chapter Five

Worry knotted Jacob's stomach as he finished reading the notes from the original investigation. Over the
past five years, he and his deputy had spoken with Cora
countless times.

They'd also received at least three complaints from
women who claimed Cora was stalking their child. All
were newer residents who'd moved to the area and had
little girls the same age as Cora's daughter.

He'd heard gossip in town about her being unstable,
but he didn't want to believe it. Although if his own
child was missing, he'd probably go crazy with rage
and fear himself.

His deputy called to confirm that he was canvass-
ing local residents for information on Philips. Jacob
was on the phone with ballistics when the front door
squeaked open.

Cora stuck her head in the doorway, and he waved
her in.

"Gun was a .38," the lab analyst said.

Jacob thanked him and turned his attention toward
Cora. She looked shaken and nervous, although that was
nothing new. She always looked as if the threads of her
faith and sanity were slowly unraveling.

Except when she was teaching. He'd visited the school a few times for safety programs and seen her with the children. She was animated, sweet, funny and loving with her kindergarteners.

A natural with children.

Jacob stood and offered Cora coffee, but she declined. Vera, his receptionist, arrived and Jacob said good morning. "Let's go back to my private office," he told Cora.

Cora followed him down a hallway into his office. "I brought those sketches," she said.

He shuffled some folders on his desk, moving them out of the way, and she sank into the chair facing his desk. Her hand was trembling as she removed an envelope from her purse.

He narrowed his eyes. "Are you okay?"

She nodded, although her forced smile didn't quite meet her eyes.

Maybe she was just upset about Kurt. Or about lying. "Something you want to tell me?" he asked.

She bit her bottom lip, then shook her head. "I labeled the sketches with the age projection."

He accepted the envelope, then removed the pages. His heart squeezed at her detailed depictions.

She'd included at least three sketches per year, starting from her memory of her infant daughter to Alice at six months, then nine, then a year. She'd added wisps of hair and chubby cheeks and a pudgy belly as a toddler, then slowly captured the changes from toddler to kindergarten.

"These are amazing," he said softly. "You're talented."

A blush stained her cheeks. "I figured you'd think I was crazy for doing them."

His gaze locked with hers. "I don't think you're crazy," he said. She was just a mother who missed her child.

He tapped the latest sketches, when Alice would have been four, then five. "I'm sending the more recent ones over. Maybe they'll be of help to the FBI."

CORA DIDN'T KNOW why she cared about Jacob's opinion, but she did. Over the years, he'd always been kind and understanding. And he had tried to find Alice.

The memory of that car on her tail taunted her.

She couldn't shake the feeling that someone had been following her. Watching her.

That she might be in danger.

She considered telling him but didn't want him to think she was paranoid.

"Cora, I spoke with Kurt Philips's ex-wife last night."

Her heart stuttered. "I'm sure she was upset about her husband's death."

"She was." Jacob's eyes narrowed on her. Studying. Probing. "She claims she hadn't talked to him in a few days."

"Did she have any idea who would try to hurt him?"

Jacob shook his head. "It's possible he was working a case besides yours that landed him in trouble, but... maybe not. The firefighters recovered a phone and laptop. They're trying to retrieve data from both, but with the fire damage, it'll take time."

Cora nodded.

His eyes darkened, lingering on her face. "However, the analyst was able to retrieve some information from Philips's phone."

Cora went still, her pulse clamoring.

"Apparently the last person he called before he died was you."

She sucked in a pain-filled breath. "I didn't talk to him," she said. *Because I was upset about losing my job.* But if she admitted that, she'd have to explain the reason. Then Jacob *would* think she was unhinged.

"The IT analyst said the call didn't go through." Jacob leaned forward and looked into her eyes. "He did send you a text, though, saying that he was dropping your case."

She pressed her lips together to stifle a reaction.

"Why didn't you tell me about the text last night?" Jacob asked in a deep voice.

She shrugged. "I…didn't think it was important."

Jacob's dark brows shot upward. "I told you Kurt was murdered, and you didn't think it was important to mention that he'd dropped your case?"

She searched for a plausible explanation. "That's right. How could it matter? If he was dropping my case, it was because he'd exhausted all leads. So he obviously wasn't killed because he'd found something."

She almost wished that were the case. Not that he was killed, but that he'd found something important enough that it meant he was close to finding her daughter. Because if he'd uncovered the truth, someone else could, and her hopes weren't completely dead in the water.

"Cora, I can understand that you'd be upset with him for dropping the search."

His sympathetic tone stirred her emotions, yet the implication of where he was headed with his questions slowly dawned on her. He'd hinted at this the night before, but asking a second time indicated he considered her a person of interest.

Anger shot through her. "Sheriff, you can't possibly think I'd hurt Kurt," she said, her voice rising an octave. "When you and everyone else, including my husband, gave up on finding my daughter, Kurt stepped in to help me. I would never have hurt him."

She clenched the arm of the chair and stood, anxious to escape his scrutiny. "Now I have to go."

"One more question," Jacob said, stopping her before she could turn and leave.

She gritted her teeth. "What?"

"Mrs. Philips mentioned that Kurt wasn't just working for you, that the two of you were involved personally."

Her fingers tightened around the strap of her shoulder bag. "We were friends," she said, unable to keep the emotions from her voice. "I'm sure you're aware that I don't have many of those. Either people think I'm unstable because I won't give up looking for Alice, or like you, they look at me with suspicion." She swallowed, tears threatening. "That hurts more than anything."

"I never treated you like a suspect," Jacob said gruffly.

Her gaze met his, and she lifted her chin. "You just did." Determined not to cry in front of him, she stormed from his office.

JACOB HATED HURTING CORA, but his job required him to ask difficult questions.

He hurried after her and caught her at the door. "Cora, let's go get some coffee and talk."

Tears glistened in her eyes. He wanted to console her, but Vera was watching, so he kept his hands to himself.

"Please, it's about Drew."

Her face paled, and he thought she was going to make a run for her car, but she gave a little nod. Together they walked to the local coffee shop The Brew, and claimed a booth.

God, she looked pale and thin. "Have you eaten anything?" he asked.

She shrugged. "I wasn't hungry this morning."

"How about a pastry?"

"I suppose I could have one."

A small smile tugged at his mouth. He'd learned early on that she liked sweets, so he chose an apple pastry and a chocolate croissant and carried them to the table. She snagged the chocolate, then tore it into three pieces before taking a bite.

He inhaled his just to give her time to settle down, then took a sip of coffee. "I'm sorry I upset you, Cora, but I'm trying to find out who killed your friend. I'd think you'd want that, too."

She squeezed her eyes closed for a minute as if composing herself. "I do."

In spite of all she'd suffered, Cora was a strong woman.

"I have to consider all angles," he continued. "With the timing of his text to you, I'm going to explore the possibility that his murder is related to your case."

"But his message said he was giving up," Cora said, her expression confused.

Jacob twisted his mouth in thought. "True. And I don't want to give you false hope. But you said Kurt wouldn't give up. What if he'd found a lead, and someone killed him to keep him from telling you? The killer could have forced him to send that text or sent it to you after they killed him."

Cora's eyes widened. "I hadn't thought of that."

"Hopefully his computer will yield insight. Let's talk more about Drew."

Cora frowned and traced a finger around the rim of her coffee mug. "I don't know what more I can add. I already told you that Kurt talked to him about Alice's disappearance."

"Did Drew know you and Kurt were involved?"

Her gaze shot to his, irritation sparking in her eyes. "He knew Kurt was working for me, but like I said, we were just friends." She paused. "Besides, Drew wouldn't have cared if I met someone else. All he talked about was that I should move on like he did."

But she hadn't been able to do that.

"I know this is painful," he said gruffly, "but let's review what happened the night Alice disappeared." If someone had witnessed something at the hospital or afterward, time might be on their side. With the passage of time, sometimes witnesses felt guilty for not coming forward or remembered details they hadn't recalled in the aftermath of a trauma.

Cora sighed. "We've been over this a thousand times before."

"True, but bear with me and just focus on Drew this time. And your marriage." Directly following the kidnapping, she'd still been in love with her husband. She'd been in shock and terrified and had clung to him.

She might look back and see their relationship in a different light now.

CORA FOUGHT TO keep her emotions at bay as she relived that night once again. "I was in labor for eighteen hours, and I'd hardly slept for two days. After I gave birth, I held Alice for a few minutes, then the nurse took her for routine tests."

"And Drew was with you?"

She nodded. "He'd been anxious about work and the money when we first learned I was pregnant. But he was there for the delivery."

"He wanted to make partner?"

"Yes, he was driven and ambitious. That's one thing I admired. At first."

"What do you mean *at first*?"

She bit her lip. She hadn't meant to say that.

"Cora, you can be honest now. It's the only way to get to the truth."

"During the pregnancy, he worked such long hours and answered calls no matter where we were. He'd miss dinners and seemed so preoccupied with his clients that I wondered if he'd spend time with the baby when we brought her home."

Jacob leaned forward, eyes piercing. "During all those late nights when he said he was working, did you ever suspect he was having an affair?"

Cora's breath caught. She tried to mentally replay those months. "I didn't at the time," she admitted. "I just thought he was focused on his career."

"Was he solicitous to other women when you went out?"

Cora shook her head. "Not really," she said. "But I did wonder if I'd be raising Alice alone while he spent all his time with clients." She tapped her nails on her coffee cup. "Then she was gone and that wasn't an issue."

He'd abandoned them both.

"I'm sorry," Jacob said. "Let's get back to that night. Before the nurse took Alice for tests, what happened?"

"Drew's phone rang, and he left the room. I rocked Alice, then the nurse took her. I fell asleep a few minutes later, and when I woke up, the fire alarm was blasting."

"Do you know how long it had been since Drew left the room?"

She shrugged. "Not long. Maybe half an hour."

"That was a long phone call," Jacob commented.

She sipped her coffee. "His business calls often ran long."

Jacob made a low sound in his throat. "I know we questioned the nurse who took Alice for the tests, but was there anything about her that felt off?"

"Not at all. Lisa was a sweetheart," Cora said. "She coached me through delivery, and afterward encouraged me to rest. I remember her saying the night feedings could get rough."

"How about anyone else? Did another staff member act strangely? Maybe you saw someone lurking by the nursery."

"I didn't go out by the nursery until after the fire started," she said. "When I first arrived at the hospital, I was wheeled directly to the labor room. I was so excited about finally getting to meet my baby that all I remember are nurses and doctors bustling around."

"I understand," Jacob said softly.

He could never understand. He hadn't held his newborn in his arms and then felt the emptiness afterward when that baby was suddenly gone.

"Back to Drew," he said. "Did he tell you who phoned him?"

She strained to remember. "He didn't mention a name. But after the nurse left with Alice, I thought I heard him talking to someone outside the door. A woman. I assumed it was Lisa."

Silence stretched between them, filled with tension and stirring questions in Cora's mind.

Drew had married within months after they'd separated. Was it possible he'd been seeing someone else while they were still married? That the phone call or the woman outside the hospital room was his lover?

Chapter Six

Doubts nagged at Cora as she walked across the street to the bookstore.

She searched her memory banks and recalled little snippets of conversations with Drew during their marriage when he'd been vague about where he was going. Late-night phone calls he answered behind closed doors. Missed dinners and outings where he'd supposedly been caught up in a case.

She'd trusted him implicitly. Had been so deep into her fantasy of a family that it never occurred to her that he'd betray her.

Yet he was a lawyer, and a good one. Lying with a straight face came easy to him on the job. Why not at home?

Nausea filled her at the possibility that he might have been talking to a lover outside the hospital room only minutes after she'd delivered their child. Surely he hadn't been…

Disturbed at her train of thought, she combed through the bookstore in search of some reading material to distract her. Although she enjoyed sketching outside with a view of the river or mountain, she had her sketchpad in her bag and sometimes came here to draw and people-watch.

The bookstore had added a small café two years ago, which was a popular gathering spot for teens, seniors and parents accompanying children. Computer stations also invited clientele to linger and work or do research.

Being surrounded by books and the people in the store helped fill her lonely summer days.

Her stomach twisted. She would have a lot more of those in the future. The uncertainty was daunting. She'd have to find a job...somewhere. Doing what, though? The only thing she'd ever done was teach.

You could move, find a teaching job in a different city.

But the thought of leaving Whistler made her uneasy. The small mountain town had been her sanctuary during her pregnancy, when she wanted to get away from the city, and then after Alice had disappeared.

Voices from the children's corner drifted toward her. Unable to resist, she maneuvered the teen section until she reached the reading nook where two mothers were reading to their little ones. Three preschool children were putting on an impromptu puppet show behind the puppet stage, and a toddler was thumbing through a picture book, pressing the sound link associated with the animal pictures.

She glanced around for an empty table where she wouldn't disturb the families, then spotted Nina Fuller at a small round table, coloring with markers.

Cora's breath caught. Nina Fuller...the little girl who'd caught her eye the first day of school this past year. She and her mother had just moved to town. Nina was in kindergarten. She wore her long brown hair in a French braid today. A slight sprinkling of freckles dotted the bridge of her nose, and her shy, sweet smile was infectious.

She was also the reason Cora had been fired.

Cora ordered herself to walk away. If Nina's mother saw her—

"Ms. Reeves!" Nina jumped up, ran toward her and threw her arms around her waist.

Emotions swirled inside Cora. She stooped down and hugged the little girl. Nina smelled like peppermint and felt like an angel. Cora squeezed her eyes shut for a moment, savoring the sweetness of the child's hug.

"Let my daughter go."

The sound of Nina's mother's voice made Cora tense. She patted Nina's back, then gave her another squeeze and slowly pulled away. "Hi, Mrs. Fuller—"

The woman's glare cut her off. She clasped her daughter's little arm. "Honey, get your coloring stuff. We have to go."

"But Mommy," Nina cried. "I wanna stay and talk to Ms. Reeves."

Cora gave the mother an imploring look. "I'm sorry if I—"

"Stay away from me and my daughter." Faye quickly gathered their belongings and rushed Nina from the store.

JACOB STUDIED THE drawings Cora had left. Doubt had filled her eyes as she recounted her relationship with Drew. She was second-guessing her husband now.

If Drew had been cheating on Cora, it changed everything. It also meant he'd lied to the police, which launched him to the top of Jacob's suspect list again.

Knowing Cora would be sentimental about the drawings, he made copies on the machine at his office, placed the originals back inside her envelope and stowed them in his desk to return to her.

Then he drove to the FBI's local field office to see Liam. Sympathy softened the hard planes of his brother's face as he examined the drawings.

"She's really talented," Liam said.

"I agree. She created composites of her childhood photographs along with her ex-husband's to project what Alice might look like today."

"This is a long shot," Liam said. "But I'll see what we can do with them." He stood. "Come on, there's something I want you to see."

Liam was short on words but quick on ideas. Like a dog with a bone when he was investigating a case, he didn't give up until he had answers. And they both wanted to find their father's killer and make him pay.

Jacob followed Liam into a room housing three analysts. "I retrieved some of the original security tapes from the hospital fire," Liam said. "Some were damaged, of course."

"We've been through these before," Jacob said, hoping Liam had something new.

"But technology has improved. Angie recovered some blurred images and cleaned them up." Liam gestured toward a female analyst whose long blond hair was in a twist at the nape of her neck.

Angie angled her monitor to review the images on her screen. "I've searched all the tapes. Frankly, they're difficult to watch," she said with a pained sigh. "So much chaos and so many terrified people. But then—" she held up a finger "—I started focusing on anyone

who looked out of place. And this caught my attention."
She clicked a key and scrolled through several frames.
"Most everyone is running toward the exits and stair-
wells." She displayed footage of two women running
toward the nursery. A dark-haired woman was quickly
ushered toward the stairs. Then Cora.

Both were terrified and frantic as they ran to save
their newborns.

Emotions clogged Jacob's throat. Watching Cora suffer made him want to pound something.

"This is Cora Reeves," Angie said. "She's obviously
trying to find her baby."

"Which confirms her story and puts her in the clear,"
Jacob said, although he'd never doubted her. A mother's
pain was a palpable force.

"Do you see the father anywhere?"

She scrolled through more footage until Jacob
pointed out Drew Westbrook. He was on the phone,
head bent, heading down the hall toward the cafeteria.

"After this, we lose him," Angie said. "But I thought
this was interesting."

Jacob leaned closer as she flipped through several
more frames, then zeroed in on a person in scrubs,
head and face not visible, carrying a bundle toward the
housekeeping area on the bottom floor.

"We thought someone took the baby during the commotion outside the hospital, but this bundle could be
Cora's baby."

Jacob narrowed his eyes, hunting for identifying
markers. Hairstyle or color. A scar. A limp. But whoever
it was had shielded his or her face from the cameras.

"Body size and height indicate it's either a small man
or a woman," Liam said.

"And that the baby was kidnapped while still inside the hospital," Jacob added.

Liam folded his arms. "We're looking into people who lost babies around that time. We also have to consider that this kidnapping could have been professional. I've been investigating a case of baby snatchers who're selling the babies."

Jacob's blood ran cold.

If that was the case, Cora's daughter could be anywhere.

CORA WATCHED WITH a heavy heart as Nina and her mother left the bookstore. The last thing she wanted to do was to frighten a child or her mother.

For goodness' sake, her former best friend had once accused her of behaving like a stalker when she'd chased down a woman in the mall pushing a baby stroller. That day, she'd been certain the woman had Alice.

Just like she'd thought Nina was her daughter when she'd seen her at school.

Terrified she was losing her mind and on the verge of another breakdown, she phoned her therapist, Ruby Denton, and requested an emergency session. The woman agreed to see her in an hour, so she forced herself to comb the bookstore for reading material. Meditation tapes had worked well to calm her. So had books of faith and stories of individuals who'd overcome tragedies to turn their lives around or use the trauma as inspiration to help others.

She selected a couple of autobiographies of survivors, one of abuse and the other, of a terrible, crippling accident. Then she chose a book on artistic styles along with a book on police sketch artists.

She paid for her purchases, then drove to Ruby's office. Her mind kept replaying the incident at the bookstore with Nina while she waited for the therapist to see her.

Finally Ruby opened her door and invited her into her office. Today the perky redhead wore a dark green suit that accentuated her eyes. She was slightly younger than Cora, and was compassionate and straightforward. An old soul, Cora thought.

As usual, she set a bottle of water on the coffee table for Cora, and they faced each other. Cora sat on a plush gray velvet love seat and Ruby in a dark red velvet wing chair.

"Tell me what's going on," Ruby said.

Cora twisted the cap off the water bottle and took a sip, then breathed out to steady her nerves. "I think I may be going crazy," she blurted.

Ruby's look softened. "I doubt that, Cora. But you're obviously upset. What happened?"

Cora explained about Nina and Faye Fuller's complaint to the principal.

"Ah, Cora," Ruby said. "I know you love teaching."

"I do," she admitted. "But maybe I overstepped. I frightened the little girl and her mother." She reiterated her encounter at the bookstore. "I didn't mean to upset them, but Nina hugged me and I couldn't help it. She's such a sweetheart that I hugged her back."

"We never know what someone else is going through," Ruby said. "You can't blame the mother for being protective."

Cora shook her head. "No, I can't. I…had no idea she'd had a miscarriage, much less three." Her voice choked. "I…do feel badly for her."

"Then tell her," Ruby said.

"I tried, but she told me to stay away from them."

A heartbeat of silence stretched between them. "Give her some time," Ruby advised. Cora twisted her fingers together, rubbing them in a nervous gesture.

"I sense something else is bothering you, Cora," Ruby said.

Cora heaved a wary breath. "I told you before about Kurt Philips, the private investigator I hired to find Alice."

"Yes. As I recall, the two of you are friends." Ruby offered her a smile. "I hope you're not feeling guilty about finding a little joy in your life."

"We were just friends," Cora said. "But…the problem is… Kurt is dead."

Another heartbeat of silence. Ruby crossed her legs, her expression concerned. "What happened?"

"He left me a message saying he was ending the search for Alice, and I should move on. I was upset and drove to Kurt's to talk to him, but when I arrived, his apartment and office were on fire." She took a breath. "Later, the sheriff told me Kurt was murdered."

Emotions overcame her, and she burst into tears.

Ruby pushed a box of tissues toward her. She waited patiently, giving Cora time to compose herself, and then asked, "Are you crying because you love Kurt and are upset about his death, or because he was dropping the search for Alice?"

Grief and anger knotted Cora's insides. "I don't know. Maybe both."

Ruby gave a small nod. "That's fair. Does the sheriff know who killed him?"

"Not yet," Cora said. "It's possible he was murdered because of me."

Ruby's eyes widened slightly. "You can't blame yourself, Cora."

"I know. But if he was killed because of my case, maybe he'd found something," Cora said, hope fighting through her anguish.

"I'm sure the sheriff will get to the truth." Ruby waited a second, then spoke softly.

"We broached this subject before. But have you thought about what you'd do if you found Alice and she's happy and in a loving home? Would you uproot her world to tell her that you're her mother?"

Chapter Seven

Anger seized Cora at the question. "You think I'm selfish for wanting to find my little girl?"

"I didn't say that," Ruby said in the calming voice that sometimes worked on Cora's last nerve. "I just want you to be prepared for whatever you find. It's been five years. I understand your pain and your need to be honest and connect with Alice if you find her. But she's not a baby anymore. If she is in a happy home and has loving parents, which I'm sure you want to be the case, learning the truth is bound to be upsetting."

Cora clutched the arm of the chair with a white-knuckled grip in an effort to keep from shouting. "And what if she's not happy? What if she's been bounced around from one foster home to another?" Cora's voice rose an octave. "Or what if whoever has her has mistreated her?" The very idea nauseated her.

"Then she'll definitely be better off if you step in." Ruby leaned forward. "I'm not being judgmental, Cora. You're in a very difficult situation, and if I were you, I'd want to know what happened to my child. You've been robbed of precious moments, of five years of her life. I'm simply trying to prepare you for whatever happens, so you can cope."

"I'm tired of coping," Cora admitted. "I've been coping for years. I need to know where she is. And I…need to hold her. To hug her. To let her know that I love her."

"But you're feeling desperate because Kurt was going to give up, aren't you?" Ruby asked.

"That's just it," Cora said. "Kurt wouldn't give up. He told me once that he never dropped a case without answers."

"But you said he left you a message."

"He did, but Kurt was murdered shortly after he sent the text. The sheriff suggested someone could have forced him to send me that message before they killed him."

Ruby narrowed her eyes. "Does the sheriff have any proof or any idea who killed Kurt?"

Cora's lungs strained for air. "Actually we talked about the day Alice was taken, and I remembered something."

Ruby shifted in her chair, interest flaring across her face. "Go on."

Cora bit her bottom lip. She felt like she was betraying Drew by reiterating her conversation with Jacob. Yet, she wanted answers and that meant probing every detail of that horrible day.

"Cora?"

"Drew received a phone call after Alice was born, and he left the room. Just as I was drifting to sleep, I heard him talking to a woman outside the door." She stood and began to pace. "I assumed it was a nurse, but the sheriff's questions started me thinking that perhaps it wasn't a nurse."

"I don't understand," Ruby said.

"I told you before Drew wasn't thrilled when he first

learned about the pregnancy, that he was worried about money and his job." Was it possible that Drew hadn't wanted Alice?

"What are you saying, Cora?"

She halted, her body tight with agitation. "During the pregnancy, he was inattentive and distracted. He constantly worked late and took late-night calls."

"You think Drew was having an affair?" Ruby asked softly.

Did she? Cora shrugged. "I don't want to believe that he'd betray me. But…if he was seeing someone else, he might have viewed the baby as an obstacle to leaving me. As long as we had her, he would be tied to me."

Having Alice kidnapped would have solved that problem.

AFTER LEAVING LIAM at the FBI's local field office, Jacob drove to Drew Westbrook's house.

Judging from the ritzy neighborhood and half-million-dollar homes set on estate lots, Cora's ex had done very well financially. The house was a two-story brick Georgian home with massive columns and an impressive view of the sprawling lake.

Jacob would never be able to afford a place like this on his salary. Not that he wanted to. He liked his cozy cabin, the mountains, the river, and the peace and quiet nature afforded.

He parked in front of the house in the circular drive, then strode to the front door and rang the bell. While he waited, he scanned the property. Professionally maintained lawn with topiary shrubs, a rose garden to the side and bench seating by the lake.

Voices from inside echoed through the doorway,

then the door opened and Drew Westbrook stood on the other side. He was dressed in gray slacks and a button-collared shirt as if he might be on his way to the office.

Surprise flared in his eyes when he spotted Jacob. "Sheriff Maverick?"

"Hello, Mr. Westbrook."

"Who is it, honey?" Drew's wife Hilary appeared as she came down the winding staircase.

"It's the sheriff of Whistler," Drew said.

Hilary's heels clicked on the marble floor as she sauntered toward them. Her emerald green pantsuit looked as if it was made of silk, and diamonds glittered on her fingers and around her neck.

"May I come in?" Jacob asked.

A sliver of hope sparked in Drew's eyes. "Do you have news about Alice?"

Hmm. Maybe he was wrong about Drew and he really had cared about his daughter. "Not exactly."

Drew's jaw tightened with worry. "Then it's about Cora?"

"What has she done now?" Hilary asked.

Jacob swung his gaze toward Drew's wife, surprised by her tone.

"Let me come in and I'll explain." He stepped into the foyer, which was decorated with expensive paintings and vases.

Drew scraped a hand through his hair, upending the neat strands, then led Jacob to a family room with leather furniture and wood accents. A small corner filled with a kid's table and books was the only indication that a child lived here. He'd forgotten Drew Westbrook had a son a year younger than his daughter would have been.

Jacob seated himself on the leather sofa, then Drew claimed a recliner facing him while Hilary sank into a plush club chair beside him. Both looked anxious as if expecting bad news.

"What's this about?" Drew asked.

Jacob folded his hands together. "Mr. Westbrook, do you know a man named Kurt Philips?"

Drew went still, and Hilary lifted a small pillow and hugged it to her.

"We've met," Drew said stiffly. "He was working for Cora."

"Was?" Jacob asked.

Drew's brows rose. "Yeah. He stopped by and questioned me a few times."

"He was not a pleasant man," Hilary interjected.

Jacob tilted his head toward the woman. He supposed some men found her attractive, but her perfect makeup, designer clothes and smile seemed fake. "You didn't like him, Mrs. Westbrook?"

She stiffened as if she realized she might have said the wrong thing. "I didn't like the way he came here asking questions about Drew, treating him like he was a suspect in his daughter's disappearance. He practically accused Drew of hiring someone to have his baby kidnapped." She scoffed and rolled her eyes. "Everyone who knows Drew will testify that he's a caring and loving man and a great father."

Drew raised a hand to silence his wife. "I understand Philips was doing his job," he said. "Cora seemed to trust him and to rely on him, but I didn't appreciate his insinuations. I had enough of that with you."

Jacob supposed Drew's direct approach came with

being a defense attorney. It also meant he had a great poker face and could lie without batting an eye.

"Now, why are you asking about Kurt Philips?" Drew asked bluntly.

Jacob cleared his throat. "First, tell me where you were last night, Mr. Westbrook?"

Drew's chin went up defensively. His wife folded her arms. "Drew and I were together last night, weren't we, darling?" Hilary said.

A slight twitch of Drew's mouth was his only reaction. It also hinted of a lie.

"Is that true?" Jacob asked.

Drew gave a slight nod. "Either tell me what's going on or leave."

Rattling the polished lawyer who'd deserted Cora and broken her heart gave Jacob pleasure. "I'm asking about Kurt Philips because he's dead."

Shock—real or feigned?—darkened the man's face, while Hilary flattened her palm against her cheek in a stunned reaction.

"Dead? How?" Drew asked.

"He was murdered," Jacob said. "Shot to death actually."

"Oh my God," Hilary murmured.

"Mr. Westbrook, the bullet the medical examiner extracted from him came from a handgun. Do you own a .38?"

RUBY'S QUESTION TAUNTED Cora as she left her therapist's office and drove home. Asking her to keep quiet about being Alice's mother wasn't fair. Her heart had been ripped from her chest the day her baby had been kidnapped.

For five long years, she'd missed precious moments of her little girl's life. The only thing that had kept her going was the thought of seeing her again.

Dark clouds rolled across the sky, threatening a summer storm as she turned onto the street leading to her house.

An image of Alice crying and frightened flashed behind her eyes. What if Alice was unhappy? What if whoever had her didn't love her?

Yet on the heels of that image, she saw her daughter laughing as another mother pushed her in a swing. Alice's hair was flying in the wind, her laugh musical and angelic. The other woman was singing a children's song about five little speckled frogs and Alice was singing along.

Tears blurred Cora's eyes. She hoped her daughter was happy. Laughing. Loved. Taken care of.

Could she destroy that happiness if she found her?

Faye and Nina Fuller's house slipped into view, and she clenched her jaw. She'd find Alice first, then decide what to do.

Maybe Jacob would locate her. Liam had those sketches now…

Her pulse jumped when she spotted Nina chasing a kitten across her front yard. She couldn't help but remember Nina lining her carrot sticks up at lunch the way Cora did as a child. There were other small details that had caught her attention and seemed…familiar. Nina also tore the top off her muffin and ate it first, just as Cora always did.

You lost your job because you frightened her and her mother.

She had to make it right.

She veered into the Fullers' driveway and parked, then inhaled a deep breath as she climbed out. Nina's mother was sitting on the front porch, watching Nina play. She stood when she saw Cora.

Cora braced herself. The woman might call the cops and request a restraining order against her. Still, she had to apologize.

Nina dropped to the grassy lawn, playing with the kitty. Cora forced herself to focus on the mother.

"I told you to stay away from my child," Faye said.

Cora nodded. "I'm actually here to see you. Please, Faye, can we talk for a minute?"

Faye crossed her arms, a wariness emanating from her.

"I promise I'm not here to hurt either of you. I want to apologize."

Faye's gaze locked with hers for a moment, tension stretching between them. Finally she gave a small nod. Cora crossed the distance and climbed the steps to the porch. Faye gestured toward the chair and Cora seated herself while Faye settled back on the glider.

"I realize I frightened you," Cora said. "I never meant to do that."

Faye studied her, her silence indicating it was okay for Cora to continue.

"I'm sure you've heard that my baby was kidnapped the night I gave birth to her."

Faye's expression softened. "I heard, and I'm sorry," she said softly. "I...can't imagine how awful it's been for you."

Cora breathed out. Faye had just tossed her an olive branch.

"It has been. Sometimes I forget about other people's problems."

Faye twisted her hands together.

"I'm truly sorry, Faye. I would never intentionally hurt you or Nina. When I heard she was adopted, I couldn't help myself from asking her about it. But that was wrong." She paused and swallowed hard. "I've just been to see my therapist. She's helping me become more aware of others' feelings."

Faye glanced at Nina, then at Cora. "I suppose I can't blame you. If I lost Nina, I'd move heaven and earth to find her."

Tears pricked at Cora's eyes. "You're doing a wonderful job with her," she said sincerely.

Faye pinched the bridge of her nose. "Thank you. Nina is my life."

"I can understand that," Cora said gently.

"It hasn't always been easy. I had three miscarriages before we adopted Nina. That was so painful. Every time I got pregnant I got my hopes up, but within a few weeks, I lost the baby."

Compassion filled Cora. "I'm so sorry, Faye. That must have been devastating."

Faye nodded and wiped at her eyes. "It took a toll on my marriage, too. My husband and I stuck together for a while, but then he started drinking."

A chill swept through Cora.

"He lost his temper when he drank," she admitted. "I tried to convince him to see a counselor or join AA, but he refused. When we got Nina, I hoped things would get better, but instead, he escalated. He drank all day, stopped going to work, and then he…"

"He what?" Cora said gently.

"He hit me," Faye said in a voice so low that it was barely discernible. "Once was all, though. I left him the day after that. There was no way I'd raise a child in an abusive home."

Cora reached out and squeezed Faye's hand. "I admire you for having the courage to walk away," she said honestly. "You've been through so much, Faye. I truly am sorry for putting you through any more pain."

Faye fluttered a hand to her cheek. "I suppose I overreacted," Faye said. "My ex threatened me before I left. He swore I'd be sorry, that he'd never let me go. Since then, I've been moving around constantly so he can't find us."

Cora sucked in a breath. "Do you have a protective order against him?"

Faye nodded. "But twice he sent people looking for me. That's the reason I freaked out when you asked Nina about the adoption. I…"

"You thought I was asking for him?"

"Yes," Faye said. "No, I don't know what I thought. I just panicked. I couldn't take the chance on him finding me or taking Nina to get back at me."

Chapter Eight

Goose bumps skated up Cora's arms. "Don't worry, Faye. You're not alone now. If you need anything, you can call me. And you should let Sheriff Maverick know what's going on. Whistler is a small town. He can keep an eye out in case a stranger comes around asking questions."

Faye wiped at her eyes again. "Thank you, Cora. I'm sorry I was so hard on you. I was just scared. I'd do anything to protect Nina."

"I understand," Cora said softly. "Your secret is safe with me."

"I appreciate that," Faye said. "Nina doesn't even remember him, and I don't want her upset."

"Of course." Nina looked up at them, noticed Cora and gave a small wave. "She's a good student, Faye. You should be proud of her."

Faye angled her head toward Cora. "I didn't mean to get you fired, Cora. I'll call the principal and talk to him."

Cora considered her offer. "Thanks. But I'm not sure it would help. He was pretty adamant that I need a break." She hesitated. "Maybe he's right. Maybe I should take a year off and clear my head, get a job doing something besides teaching." Where she wasn't tortured every day by taking care of other people's children.

Although she had no idea what she would do. She enjoyed working with kids. Their optimism and exuberance for life had brightened her darkest days.

"Well, let me know if you change your mind," Faye offered.

"What about you?" Cora asked. "Are you working this summer?"

Faye fidgeted. "I sell real estate at Whistler Mountain Realty, so I'll work some. But Nina can go with me."

Nina ran up, hugging the kitty to her. "Look, Ms. Reeves, Mama said we can keep her."

"That's wonderful. Kittens are so much fun." Cora smiled at the sight of the little girl hugging the fluffy yellow butterball in her arms.

"I wants a dog, too," Nina said, "but Mama says we move too much to keep a dog." She stroked the kitten's head. "I like it here. I hope we don't move anymore."

Faye hugged Nina. "We'll see, sweetheart. For now, we're staying put."

"Goody!" Nina bounced up and down. "'Cause I wanna wade in the creek out back and swim in the pond, and maybe we could go camping and sleep in a tent!"

Faye laughed. "I don't know about the tent, but we'll definitely go wading and swimming now it's getting warmer."

"Can Ms. Reeves go with us?" Nina asked.

Faye's mouth tightened slightly, and Cora stood. She'd pushed it enough for the day.

"Thank you for asking," she told Nina. "Maybe one day we can all do something together. But I have to go now."

"Okay. See you later." Nina dropped to the ground again with the kitten, sprawled on her back and set the kitten on her belly. Her laughter echoed in Cora's ears and sent a fresh pang of longing through Cora as she said goodbye to Faye and returned to her car.

JACOB STUDIED DREW and Hilary Westbrook, searching for underlying meanings to the looks they exchanged. He'd never liked Drew, and he didn't care for his wife, either.

"No, Sheriff Maverick, I do not own a gun," Drew said. "And as I stated before, I had nothing to do with my daughter's kidnapping. I'd give anything to find her. And if Kurt Philips had a lead, I certainly wouldn't have hurt him." Emotions strained his face. "I love my wife and son," he said. "But Cora is still suffering and can't move on. I want us to find Alice, so she can finally be happy again."

Jacob raised a brow. That statement was the most sincere thing he'd ever heard Drew Westbrook say. Not that he hadn't been upset after the kidnapping. He had.

His emotional pleas on TV and in the newspapers had garnered sympathy from everyone who'd seen his tears.

"When was the last time you spoke to Philips or saw him?" he asked.

"It's been months," Drew said. "He stopped by my office one day and accused me of using my daughter's kidnapping to further my career." He squared his shoulders. "I can assure you I didn't need to do that. I'm good at my job. That's the reason I earned my promotion."

"He is," Hilary spoke up again. "Don't get me wrong," Hilary said. "My heart goes out to Cora. I tried to be her friend after the kidnapping, but she pushed me away. Then she had a breakdown." Hilary toyed with the diamond dangling from a gold chain around her neck. "One time she chased another mother at the mall and nearly snatched her child from her baby stroller."

Jacob gritted his teeth. Unfortunately, he had heard similar rumors.

"One of our friends was with her, and tried to convince her to leave the woman alone. Cora started screaming, and security came and had to escort her out of the mall."

"Hilary," Drew chided in a low voice.

"Well, it's true," Hilary said. "For heaven's sake, she drove all her friends away."

Jacob's protective instincts for Cora rose to the surface. Cora had gotten under his skin five years ago when he'd first met her. The two of them had been in shock and devastated over their individual losses. "Everyone deals with stress and traumatic events in their own way."

"Maybe so," Hilary conceded. "But poor Cora was obsessed. If that PI decided to give up, no telling what Cora would do."

"I've already talked to Cora," Jacob said. "I don't believe she'd hurt him."

Hilary started to speak again, but Drew laid his hand on his wife's arm. "Hilary, that's enough. This has been stressful on all of us."

Hilary offered her husband a sympathetic look. "I'm sorry, Drew. Of course you're right." She turned to Jacob. "I apologize, Sheriff. I didn't mean to speak ill of Cora. I really want her to find some peace. If I lost our little boy, I'd probably break down, too."

"There's something else," Jacob said, knowing the couple wouldn't like his questions, but he had to ask. "Mr. Westbrook, Cora remembers hearing you talking to a woman outside the hospital room before the fire started. Whom were you talking to?"

Confusion marred the man's face. "I...don't remember. Probably the nurse."

Jacob tilted his head toward Hilary. "I understand you worked with Drew prior to his divorce."

Hilary shifted. "I did. I was his administrative assistant."

He turned back to Drew. "Mr. Westbrook, I know you were stressed about the baby and your job, and that you were working late hours."

Drew's eyes narrowed to slits. "I was new at the firm and trying to impress the partners."

"Was that all there was to those nights?" Jacob asked. "Or were you having an affair?"

JACOB'S QUESTIONS ABOUT Drew taunted Cora as she stopped by the arts and crafts store on the way back to her house. Had Drew cheated on her?

The first few days and weeks after the kidnapping were a blur. Drew had seemed sincerely upset about Alice.

He could have had an affair and still been upset over the kidnapping. But if he was seeing another woman and wanted out of their marriage, and had been involved in Alice's disappearance, maybe he'd faked his reaction.

Tormented by the idea that he would betray her, her lungs strained for air. She practiced deep breathing for a few minutes in the car to steady her nerves, then went inside the store.

She needed more art paper, another sketchbook for her drawings, paints and a couple of canvases.

With time on her hands in the summer, she typically enjoyed working on art projects. Anything to distract her from obsessing over Alice.

Anything to help her hold on to her sanity.

There had been a time when she'd considered taking her own life, when living had been so painful that she could barely get out of bed. But the idea of Alice searching for her when she got older, then discovering her mother had killed herself forced Cora to banish that thought from her head.

If—no, *when*—she found her daughter, she wanted Alice to know she was strong and that she'd never given up looking for her.

On the off chance that Faye and Nina actually visited her someday, she picked up a small art set for children she thought Nina would enjoy. The kit included color pencils, crayons, paints, markers and charcoal.

Her heart stuttered at the image of Nina opening the set and pulling out the supplies.

Stop it, she chided herself. Faye had been cordial, but that didn't mean she wanted to be friends.

She paid for the supplies, carried them to her car, then drove through town. In spite of the dark clouds above, mothers and children were at the park, triggering another wave of longing.

She checked for Jacob's SUV as she passed the sheriff's office but didn't see it, so she headed home. A few raindrops began to splatter against her window. She flipped on the windshield wipers and slowed as she rounded a curve.

The sound of a car engine rumbled behind her, and

she remembered thinking she was being followed earlier. Instinctively she slowed and turned into the first drive she saw, then waited until the car moved on.

Breathing out in relief, she backed up, then sped toward her house. But just as she rounded another curve near the turnoff for the river park, a popping sound echoed, then the glass window on the passenger side suddenly shattered.

Another pop and Cora screamed as a bullet zoomed by her head.

She quickly ducked, but her car skidded toward the embankment. She swerved to the right and braked, but her tires squealed and she slammed into the guardrail. Metal clanged and screeched, and her car nose-dived into the ditch.

She tried to brace herself for the impact, but her head snapped back, more glass shattered and she was thrown forward. The airbag exploded, slamming into her, and pain ricocheted through her chest.

Then stars swam behind her eyes as darkness swallowed her.

JACOB STUDIED WESTBROOK'S REACTION.

The lawyer fisted his hands on his chair arms. "I most certainly was not having an affair. I never cheated on Cora, and I resent the implication."

"Is that what she told you?" Hilary screeched.

Jacob shook his head. "No, but under the circumstances I had to ask."

"We went through all this when Alice was first kidnapped." Drew stood and gestured toward the door. "I was treated like a suspect then, and I get the distinct feeling the same thing is happening now. If you have more questions, Sheriff, go through my attorney."

Jacob stood and adjusted his holster. "I can do that if necessary. But if you want to find your daughter, you'll cooperate."

"I have cooperated and told you everything I know." Drew headed toward the entry, and Jacob followed. "If that private investigator was killed because he uncovered information about my daughter, I want to know."

Drew was definitely sending out mixed messages. One moment he genuinely seemed to care about Cora and finding Alice.

The next second, he was lawyering up. The timing of his success seemed suspicious, too. Thanks to media coverage, he'd vaulted to the top of his career in record time after the kidnapping. He'd married within a year after he and Cora separated and had another child.

He also had access to any number of criminals who would kill for him for money or in exchange for a better deal in court.

Jacob stood on the steps to the house for a minute after Drew closed the door, listening for the couple's voices in case they argued, but he didn't hear them.

He jogged down the steps, climbed in his SUV and decided to stop by Liam's office before heading back to Whistler. He called Griff on the way.

"Any word on the computer you retrieved from Philips's office?" he asked gruffly.

"The analyst is working on retrieving files. He thinks he might have something by tomorrow."

"Good." Jacob relayed his conversation with the Westbrooks. "If the PI found a lead about the Reeves-

Westbrook baby kidnapping, we need to know what it was."

"I'll keep you posted." Griff hesitated. "There's something else. I've been checking arson cases similar to the hospital fire and found a couple that are similar. One was at a school and the other at a mall. I'm going to talk to the officers who investigated those cases."

"Which means the fire wasn't a setup for the kidnapping?"

"Right," Griff admitted. "We have to explore every angle. True arsonists are thrill seekers who enjoy the thrill of the fire and the chaos that follows."

Jacob gritted his teeth as he hung up. He'd never understand how anyone took pleasure in another person's pain. But Griff was right.

If the hospital fire was caused by a thrill seeker, whoever took Cora's baby may have done so on the spur of the moment, a crime of opportunity. That would also explain why there was never a ransom note or they hadn't found anyone lurking by the nursery watching the newborns prior to the fire.

He stewed over that as he drove to the FBI headquarters. He and Liam spent another hour reviewing security tapes again. Liam pointed out two baby kidnappings he suspected were related to a kidnapping ring.

Finally Jacob headed back to Whistler, the miles clicking away. The temptation to stop by Cora's struck him, but he ordered himself to drive home.

He could not get personally involved with Cora. She was vulnerable and needed answers, not for him to get romantically involved with her. Not that she would be interested…

He turned onto Main Street when his phone buzzed. His deputy. He immediately connected.

"Jacob, it's Martin. A 911 call just came in. There was a wreck on Route 9, a red Ford Escape."

Jacob's blood ran cold. Cora drove a red Ford Escape.

Chapter Nine

Jacob pressed the accelerator. Cora had been in an accident.

Dear God, let her be all right.

He swung the police SUV around, flipped his siren on and sped toward Route 9. Thankfully traffic was minimal. Another plus to living in a small town—people actually paid attention when he appeared and pulled over to let him pass. His heart pounded with fear as he rounded a curve and spotted the guardrail dented and skid marks on the pavement where Cora had careened off the road.

Emergency workers hadn't arrived yet, and he willed them to hurry as he pulled to the side of the road and jumped out. The front of Cora's SUV was in the ditch, smoke billowing from the rear.

He jumped over the guardrail, his boots skidding in the dirt, gravel and rocks flying as he rushed down the incline. His heart hammered at the sight of the shattered driver's window.

The acrid smell of smoke hit him as it seeped from the rear of the car.

A reminder he had to hurry.

He peered inside the window. The airbag had deployed. He pulled his knife from his pocket and tried to open the door, but the corner was stuck in the ditch.

Dammit.

"Cora," he shouted. "Honey, can you hear me?"

Nothing.

Fear pulsed through him. He ran back to his SUV, grabbed a shovel from the trunk and flew back down the hill to the car. He dug dirt from the door then pried it open it so he could reach Cora. With a quick jab of his knife, he ripped the airbag.

Cora moaned. Thank God she was alive. "Hang in there, Cora. Rescue workers are on their way."

A siren wailed, and he stroked her shoulder, hoping she could hear him as he murmured reassurances. He didn't dare move her until the medics arrived.

The siren grew louder, then tires screeched. He glanced up the hill. An ambulance and fire engine roared to a stop. Jacob waved the workers down the hill.

"What do we have?" one of the firemen asked.

"Woman, driver, name is Cora Reeves. Airbag deployed. She's unconscious but alive."

Jacob leaned into the car. "Cora, the medics are here."

She moaned softly and started to lift her head. "Stay still, ma'am," one of the medics said. "We'll have you out in a minute."

She murmured "Okay," and Jacob stepped aside while emergency workers cut Cora's seat belt, then braced her neck before easing her from the vehicle and boarding her. He followed them up the hill to the ambulance and stood beside her while the medic called the hospital.

Jacob cradled her hand in his, disturbed at her ice-cold skin. "Cora?"

She blinked and opened her eyes, squinting as if her head hurt. "Jacob—"

"Shh, it's all right. You had a car accident, but you'll be fine." At least he hoped to hell she would.

"Not...accident," she said in a raw whisper.

"Yes, you had an accident and ran off the road," he said softly.

She shook her head. "No...*no* accident."

Jacob froze. "What do you mean, no accident?"

She swallowed as if her voice wouldn't quite work.

"Cora?"

"Someone...shot at me."

Jacob's blood turned to ice. "You're sure?"

She nodded. "Hit window..."

He muttered a silent curse.

The medic cleared his throat. "We're ready to transport her."

Jacob squeezed Cora's hand. "Did you see who it was?"

She shook her head.

"We really need to go," the medic said.

Jacob thumbed a strand of hair from Cora's cheek. "I'll see you at the hospital. I'm going to take a look at your car."

Cora's eyes drifted closed as they loaded her into the ambulance.

Jacob hurried to his SUV and retrieved his evidence kit, then raced back down the hill to comb the car and area for forensics.

CORA'S HEAD WAS still swimming as the medics pushed her into the ER. On the drive to the hospital, she'd tested her limbs and was grateful she could move her legs. She didn't think anything was broken, either.

Thank heavens for the airbag. It had probably saved her life.

The attending physician conducted a preliminary exam. "Everything looks clear," Dr. Pattinson told her. "I'm ordering chest X-rays to look for broken ribs and a CAT scan in case you have a concussion."

Cora hated hospitals. The last time she was admitted was when her daughter was stolen.

"Can I go home after that?" Cora asked.

"Let's see how the tests turn out," he said. "We might keep you here for observation overnight."

The image of flames and smoke taunted her. She couldn't stay here tonight. "No, I have to go home," Cora said.

The memory of the bullet whizzing by her head flashed behind her eyes as a technician rolled her to the imaging center.

She was lucky to be alive. But fear tightened every muscle in her body.

Someone had tried to kill her. And she wanted to know the reason why.

DAYLIGHT WAS WANING. The dark clouds robbed any remaining sunlight, casting the area in gray. Jacob tugged on latex gloves and used a flashlight to examine the car, starting with the shattered windows.

Glass littered the interior of the front seat and floor. A bullet hole made him curse. Cora was right. This was no accident.

He snapped photographs with his phone, then opened the passenger door and shined the light inside in search of a bullet casing.

He walked the area, looking at the vehicle from all

angles to estimate the trajectory of the bullet and the shooter's origin.

Judging from the evidence, the bullet had come from the passenger side.

He searched the floorboard and found a partial casing amongst the shattered glass. Next he moved to the driver's side and examined that window. Evidence of another bullet skimming the glass indicated it had traveled through the passenger window and across the car, close to Cora's head. He shined the light across the interior of the door, the ceiling and roof and spotted the bullet lodged in the roof where it met the window casing. Cursing, he used his knife to dig it out and bagged it with the other casing.

Anger railed through him. Except for frightening a few nervous mothers over the years, Cora had never hurt anyone in her life.

But she had been relentless in pushing to keep her case on police radar. And then she'd hired that PI.

Which pointed to a motive. Someone was afraid Cora was about to uncover the truth about the kidnapping.

And that person—the kidnapper—was close by.

Maybe even in Whistler.

He or she was watching Cora.

Jacob turned and scanned the area. Thick woods backed up to the ditch where the shooter could have hidden. The shooter could have been in another car, though, waiting until just the right moment to open fire.

Perspiration beaded on the back of his neck as adrenaline kicked in. He grabbed his phone, called his deputy to explain the situation and asked Martin to meet him at the scene.

When he hung up, Jacob combed the ground in

case the shooter had snuck up to the car while Cora was unconscious. He shined his flashlight across the ground and embankment looking for footprints, a piece of clothing that might have snagged on a twig, a button, cigarette, anything that might point to the shooter's identity.

But the only footprints he found were his own. No clothing or anything that might have belonged to the shooter.

A few minutes later, Martin drove up and met him by the car. "Search the woods for forensics in case the perp parked and hid behind the trees before or after he ambushed Cora." He handed the bullet casings to his deputy to courier to the lab just as the tow truck arrived. "Before they move the car, see if you find prints on the door. Mine will be there and Cora's, but it's possible the perp slipped up to see if Cora was alive."

"Copy that," his deputy said.

"Who made the 911 call?" Jacob asked.

"I believe Cora did," Martin said.

She must have regained consciousness long enough to phone for help, then lost consciousness again.

"I'm going to the hospital," Jacob said. "Maybe she saw the shooter or his car."

Fear gripped him as he headed to his vehicle. He had to hurry.

If the shooter knew Cora had survived, he or she might come after her again.

CORA HATED THE hospital sounds and smells.
After the CAT scan, she was wheeled back to the ER.

Her clothes were torn and bloody from the glass fragments that had pelted her arm, so the nurses gave her a pair of scrubs to wear home. Her wrist was bruised and swollen; a small butterfly bandage covered the cut on her forehead at her hairline, and her ankle was wrapped.

It seemed like hours before the doctor appeared with her results. "Thankfully nothing appears to be broken, so that's good." He offered her a sympathetic smile. "The CAT scan looks clean, too. I'd say you were a lucky lady today."

She would hardly call being shot at lucky. But she was alive.

A nurse poked his head into the room. "Sheriff Maverick is here."

"Is it all right if he comes in?" Dr. Pattinson asked.

Cora nodded and rubbed her arms with her hands. Jacob stepped inside, his jaw clenched.

"I'm going to release you," Dr. Pattinson said. "But you should take it easy for a day or two. Do you understand, Cora?"

"Yes, thank you." She just wanted to go home and crawl into her own bed.

"I'll drive you home," Jacob offered.

Cora had no other way, so she simply murmured her thanks.

"If you experience dizziness, nausea or severe headaches, please call," Dr. Pattinson said.

"I will." Cora gripped the edge of the bed to stand.

"I'll get a wheelchair," the nurse offered.

"I don't need one," Cora protested.

Dr. Pattinson cleared his throat. "It's hospital policy."

Jacob stepped to the side of the bed to steady her, but she waved off his concern, determined to prove she was well enough to be released. One of the hospital staff members brought discharge papers, and she scribbled her signature.

A minute later, the nurse returned with the wheelchair. In spite of her bravado, her legs were weak and she was grateful for the ride. Jacob pulled his SUV up to the door, and the nurse wheeled her to the passenger side.

Jacob rushed to assist her, and seconds later, they were settled in the car and pulling from the parking lot.

Jacob gave her a look of concern. "How do you feel?"

"Tired," Cora said, struggling not to fall apart.

Jacob raised a brow. "You sure you're ready to go home?"

She blinked away a dizzy spell. "I'm sure. The last time I was in a hospital, it didn't turn out so well."

"God, Cora, I'm sorry. I should have realized."

"It's fine," she said. "But I'll sleep better in my own bed." If she slept at all.

The memory of that shooter coming out of nowhere haunted her, and she scanned the roads and side streets as they drove through town. Jacob seemed extra alert for trouble, too.

"I had your car towed to be processed for evidence," Jacob said grimly. "I found two bullet casings and am sending them to the lab."

Images of those last few minutes before she crashed flashed behind her eyes. The fear. The feeling of having lost control. The sound of metal crashing and glass shattering.

The realization that someone was trying to kill her.

"What were you doing earlier today, before the crash?" he asked.

She narrowed her eyes. "What?"

"Let's retrace your day. It's possible that someone you talked to or saw got nervous and shot at you."

She twisted her hands in her lap. His logic made sense. "After I left your office, I went to the bookstore. I ran into a little girl I knew from school and her mother."

He nodded. "Go on."

She explained about Faye getting upset over her questions at school, then warning her to stay away from Nina. "I felt bad for frightening her and Nina, so I decided to see my therapist."

He remained silent, eyes on the road.

"After that, I dropped by Faye's house to apologize."

"How did that go?"

She shrugged, the movement causing her shoulder to ache. "Actually better than I expected. We had a heart-to-heart. She told me about her miscarriages and I assured her I meant her and Nina no harm. Then I left."

A tense heartbeat passed. "Do you think she was scared enough to try to warn you off by shooting at you?"

Cora gave a little chuckle. "Heavens, no. Faye may have been nervous, but she's not dangerous. Besides, she and Nina were together when I left."

She rubbed her temple as they wove around the mountain road to her house. "But now that I think about it, twice lately, I thought someone was following me."

Jacob parked and turned toward her. "Why didn't you tell me?"

"I thought I was just being paranoid." And that he'd think she was crazy.

His expression turned grim, but he climbed from the SUV and darted around the front to her side. She was opening the door by the time he reached her. He clasped her hand as she slid out. As much as she valued her independence, she wasn't foolish enough to try to walk up her graveled drive on unsteady legs.

Thankfully he'd grabbed her purse from her car, and she retrieved her keys. Her hand was shaking, though, and she fumbled with the keys and dropped them.

Jacob picked up the keys and opened the door.

Cora sighed as they entered. "Thanks for driving me home."

He paused in the doorway and gently cradled her arms with his hands, forcing her to look at him. "Someone tried to kill you tonight. There's no way I'm leaving you alone."

A chill swept through her at his words, and the tears she'd tried to keep at bay seeped from her eyes.

Jacob pulled her up against his chest and wrapped his arms around her. It had been so long since anyone had held her or comforted her that she leaned into him and let the tears fall.

Chapter Ten

Jacob ordered himself to release Cora, but his body refused to listen to his brain. When he'd seen Cora inside that car unconscious, he'd realized something.

He cared more about her than he should.

For some odd reason, the hospital fire and the tragedies in their lives had created a bond. He'd been connected to her the moment he'd met her, when she'd looked up at him with those big, baby blue eyes and pleaded with him to find her baby.

She nestled against his chest, her body trembling. He rubbed slow circles over her back, soothing her and rocking her in his arms.

"You're safe now, Cora," he murmured against her hair. "I won't let anyone hurt you."

She nodded against his chest, then ran her hands up his back. Emotions blended with desire, making his body harden. He feathered her hair from her forehead and forced himself to pull away slightly. He had to wrangle his libido under control.

Cora needed tenderness, not a man's lust.

His own needs be damned. He'd give her what she needed.

"I can't believe this is happening," she said in a low whisper.

Jacob eased himself from her. "I'll find out who shot at you, Cora. Don't worry. He won't get away with it."

She sniffed, her body trembling again, and he took her arm and ushered her to the sofa.

"Lie down and rest. I'll fix you something to eat."

"You don't have to do that," Cora said.

"Yes, I do, it's my job to take care of Whistler's residents, and I intend to do that."

She stiffened slightly, and he sensed he'd said something wrong. Then she laid her head back against the sofa pillow and closed her eyes.

While she rested, he made himself at home in her kitchen. She must like to cook, because the pantry was stocked and so was the refrigerator. He found ingredients for a small salad and chopped lettuce, tomatoes and cucumbers. Then he noticed jars of homemade vegetable soup in the pantry, so he opened one of those, poured it into a pan and heated it up.

While it was warming, he checked on Cora. She'd dozed off, so he spread a blanket over her, turned the soup to warm, then decided to check her house for an intruder.

There were no signs of a break-in at the door or windows. He walked the property outside the house, using his flashlight to illuminate the ground, but found no footprints. At least the shooter hadn't been stalking her at home.

Although since he'd failed today, there was no telling what he'd do.

Jacob would have to convince Cora to install a security system.

By the time he went back inside, Cora was stirring from sleep. He crossed the room to her and knelt beside her. "Are you up for a meal?"

She rubbed at her forehead, her finger brushing the bandage with a frown. "That would be good."

He helped her stand, watching her carefully to make certain she wasn't dizzy. "Let me take a quick shower and change out of these scrubs," she said.

"All right. I'll keep the soup warm."

She disappeared into the bedroom, and he set the table, then walked out onto the back deck and looked out at the mountains. Anything to distract him from thinking about Cora in the shower.

Yet images of her trapped in that car taunted him. Dammit, he could use a beer right now.

But he'd stick to water.

He needed to keep a clear head to protect Cora.

CORA SPLASHED COLD water on her face and stared at herself in the mirror. Her bruises and the bandage on her forehead looked stark in the dim light.

She couldn't believe that big, strong, tough Jacob Maverick was in her kitchen cooking her dinner. It had been a long time since anyone had taken care of her. When they were first married, Drew had been attentive and had occasionally cooked. But as time passed, his attention toward work had replaced his time with her.

She stripped the scrubs, frowning at the black-and-purple skin marring her chest and legs, then forced her thoughts away from the accident. She was home now. Safe.

At least for a little while.

But Kurt was dead. And someone wanted her in the ground with him.

Trembling, she climbed in the shower and let the warm water wash away the scent of perspiration and smoke. She scrubbed her body and hair then rinsed and dried off. A quick comb through her hair and she left it damp, the strands curling around her shoulders. She dressed in an oversize T-shirt and yoga pants, then tossed the scrubs into the laundry basket.

She found Jacob standing on her back porch, staring at the mountains. She'd always loved the view and the quiet, but it struck her that she was completely isolated.

A shiver tore through her. Anyone could sneak through the woods and break in through the back door or window.

Jacob turned to look at her, and another shiver rippled through her. This time not from fear. A sensual awareness that she hadn't felt in a long time heated her blood.

Her gaze locked with his, and tension simmered between them.

"You okay?" he asked gruffly.

She nodded, although she wasn't okay. The memory of his arms and solid chest against hers made her crave the safety of his embrace again. But leaning on Jacob could become a habit.

He was only being nice because it was his job. And she needed him to do that and find her daughter more than she needed him to hold her.

He gestured toward the kitchen. "Are you ready to eat?"

Her stomach growled, and she nodded and stepped back inside. Jacob went straight to the stove and dished them up bowls of soup while she set the salad on the table. It seemed odd to be doing something so routine as to share a simple meal with Jacob.

"Thanks for making dinner," she said as she sank into the kitchen chair.

"All I did was heat it up. You made this soup and canned it?"

She shrugged. "I have a lot of time on my hands in the summer," she admitted. "Gardening is therapeutic. And I like to use fresh vegetables and herbs that I grow."

"You garden and cook and draw. Is there anything you can't do, Cora?"

Be a mother. No, she *could* do that if she hadn't lost her child.

"Cora?"

"I just want to find Alice," she said softly.

Jacob covered her hand with his. "We will. But in the meantime, we have to keep you safe. I'd like to arrange for a security system to be installed ASAP."

Cora agreed readily. It wouldn't do any good if she was dead when her little girl was found.

JACOB ATTEMPTED SMALL TALK with Cora while they ate, but he failed miserably. Asking about her plans for the summer only resurrected that haunted look in her eyes.

"I'll garden and draw and try to fill the days by helping gather donations for the food pantry at the church," she admitted.

Her unspoken words rang in his ears. *But every minute she'd be thinking of her daughter.*

"I know it's difficult, Cora, but hang in there."

Cora finished her soup and took a sip of water, then explained she'd lost her job. "I'm sure you think I'm deranged." She ran her fingers through the damp strands of her hair. Fresh from the shower and with no makeup, she looked young and sexy.

Except for that bandage on her forehead and the bruises that matched.

"I don't think you're deranged," Jacob said in a quiet tone. "I miss my father every day. Sometimes I think I've been so obsessed with finding his killer that I've forgotten to live."

Cora squeezed her eyes closed for a minute, then opened them and blinked as if battling tears. "Thank you for saying that. I see the way people look at me sometimes. I never meant to frighten Nina or her mother." She tapped her fork on the table, an odd look streaking her face.

"What is it? Did you remember something else?" Jacob asked.

Cora swallowed hard. "I promised I wouldn't say anything, Jacob, so this is confidential, but if anything happened to Nina, I'd never forgive myself."

Jacob tilted his head to the side. "What are you talking about?"

Cora sighed, the sound weighted with worry. "Faye said she left her husband, Nina's adopted father, because he was abusive. She's been moving around because he's dangerous, and she's afraid he's looking for them."

"Where is he now?"

Cora shrugged. "She didn't say. But I urged her to talk to you so you could be on the lookout in case a stranger comes to town asking about them."

Jacob gritted his teeth. Domestic violence was something he couldn't tolerate. His father taught him that being a man meant protecting women and children, not taking your anger out on them.

"I won't say anything, but I will keep my eyes and ears open," he said. "If you see her again, encourage her to talk to me."

"Thank you, Jacob."

"Just doing my job," he said. "After you left the Fuller house, what happened? Did you go anywhere else? Talk to someone? Get a phone call?"

She shook her head. "No, I was headed home when I thought someone was following me."

"Did you get a look at the car?"

"The car I saw earlier was a dark sedan. But tonight... I didn't see anything. As I was rounding a curve, the bullet hit the window." She shivered. "I braked, then another bullet flew through the glass near my head. I ducked and ran off the road, then slid into the ditch."

She cleared the table as if she needed to release nervous energy. Knowing she was sore from the accident, he took over at the sink.

"Lie down and get some rest," he murmured. "I'll finish here."

"I can do it," Cora said. "I'm sure you have other things to do."

He cleared his throat, set his salad plate down and faced her. "I'm not going anywhere tonight, Cora. Keeping you safe is my priority."

A wary look fluttered in Cora's eyes. Was she afraid of him?

He softened his tone. "Tomorrow I'll arrange to install a security system. But tonight I'll sack out on your couch to make sure whoever shot at you doesn't show up."

Panic darkened her face, and he could have kicked

himself for what he'd said. Instead of soothing her fears, he'd intensified them.

But someone had tried to kill her today.

And he didn't intend to let Cora die.

JACOB'S WORDS ECHOED in Cora's head. He thought the shooter might come to her house. She wanted to bury herself in his arms and hide until he'd found the person who wanted her dead.

But he was only doing his job. He'd made that plain and clear.

That was what she needed, though. Jacob to find the shooter and to find Alice.

She couldn't afford to imagine anything more between them, not when she was so broken.

"I'll get you a pillow and a blanket." She gathered the items from the closet and set them on the couch.

Jacob had cleaned up the dishes and now stood by the back door as if scanning her property for trouble. Nerves clawed at her, and exhaustion tugged at her, so she said good-night before she did something stupid like throw herself into his arms.

Her cell phone buzzed from her purse, and she retrieved it. Drew.

She started not to answer. But what if he'd learned something about their daughter?

She pressed Accept Call and said hello.

"Cora, what the hell are you doing sending the sheriff over to question me about your PI boyfriend?"

The anger in his tone triggered her own. "He was not my boyfriend—"

"I don't give a damn if he was, but I don't appreciate you insinuating to Sheriff Maverick that I was having an affair!" His breath rasped out. "For God's sake, you don't really think that I had something to do with our baby's kidnapping, do you?"

Cora touched the bandage on her forehead. Someone had tried to kill her. And Jacob had questioned Drew. He was certainly angry now.

He wouldn't try to kill her.

Would he?

Chapter Eleven

Anger struck Cora. "I didn't give the sheriff that idea," Cora said. "But since you brought up the subject, were you having an affair, Drew?"

"What?" His tone sounded incredulous. "I can't believe you'd ask me that."

"Why not?" she snapped. "You certainly moved on pretty quickly, both from Alice and me."

A strained silence stretched between them for a minute. When Drew finally responded, frustration thickened his voice. "That's not fair, Cora. I was hurting, too, only you were too mired in your own emotions that you didn't notice."

Cora sucked in a breath. She felt as if she'd been punched in the gut.

But today had been too frightening and upsetting for her to contemplate whether or not she'd been selfish.

Tears threatened. "I have to go." She didn't wait for a response. She ended the call and turned the phone to silent in case Drew called back.

Still, adrenaline was pumping through her, so she retrieved her stationery, then sat down at her desk to write her daughter another letter.

Dear Alice,

Today I saw a little girl named Nina at the bookstore. I met her at the school where I taught. She lays her carrot sticks out in rows like I did when I was little. She also eats the top of her muffin first.

She has pretty brown hair and a sprinkling of freckles across her nose, and she likes to draw. I'm making friends with her mother, Faye.

Maybe when I find you and you come to live with me, you and Nina can have a playdate and become friends. If you like to paint or draw, I'll buy canvasses, and we'll carry a picnic to the park by the river and the two of you can paint.

I miss you so much, my sweet little girl. I hope that I get to see you soon. Then you can tell me all about what you've been doing the past five years.

I love you always,
Mommy

A pang seized Cora as the therapist's words reverberated in her head. *What will you do if you find her and she's happy?*

She shoved the voice to the far recesses of her mind. First she'd find Alice. Then she'd decide what to do.

She carefully placed the letter in her keepsake box, then crawled into bed and flipped out the light.

But as she closed her eyes, Drew's angry words screamed in her head. Drew, who might have betrayed their marriage. Drew, who'd abandoned her after they lost Alice.

An image of Jacob stretched out on her couch flashed behind her eyes. Jacob, who was strong, steadfast, a family man. Jacob, who'd never treated her as if she was unstable. Jacob, who'd promised not to give up the search for her daughter. Jacob, who'd suffered a loss the night of the hospital fire.

But he hadn't abandoned his family because of it.

The temptation to ask him to join her in bed seized her.

She wanted his warmth. His strength.

She wanted his touch. His kiss. His hands. His mouth. His big warm body giving her pleasure.

She slipped from bed and padded to the door. She cracked it a fraction of an inch, then peeked inside her living room. But his voice echoed to her, and she realized he was on the phone.

"Don't worry, Liam, I'm not getting personally involved with Cora Reeves."

Cora's pulse jumped as disappointment filled her. Obviously her feelings for Jacob were one-sided.

Battling tears again, she closed the door, tiptoed back to bed and crawled beneath the covers, alone.

JACOB BARELY DOZED off for listening to Cora tossing and turning all night. He checked the perimeter of the house several times, but everything seemed quiet.

Perhaps the shooter thought Cora hadn't survived, and he wouldn't return. Although if Cora knew the person who'd tried to kill her, or if he was watching her, he'd know she was alive.

By dawn, he rose, made a cup of coffee and a to-do list.

As soon as he deemed it a reasonable hour, he phoned the local security company. They agreed to meet at the house at ten to install a system.

Then he tracked down the head nurse who'd worked the neonatal unit at the time of the hospital fire.

Cora opened the door, looking sleepy. Her hair was tousled, and the bruises on her face and arms were even more stark in the morning light streaming through the windows.

He dragged his eyes away from her curvy body in those pajama pants and T-shirt. The pale blue color accentuated the vivid hue of her eyes, eyes that looked wary this morning. "Did you finally get some sleep?" he asked.

She nodded. "A little. How about you?"

"A little," he admitted, although he'd been tormented by the fact that she could have died the night before. If he'd done his job and found Alice years ago, Cora wouldn't be in danger now.

She walked into the kitchen, removed a mug from the cabinet and made herself a cup of coffee.

"I heard your phone ring before bedtime," he said.

She shrugged. "Drew called."

Jacob stiffened. "What did he have to say?"

She sank into the kitchen chair. "He was furious and accused me of telling you that he had an affair."

"Any investigator would ask the same question," Jacob said. "Unfortunately in a child kidnapping, we have to look at the parents, their friends and enemies, and acquaintances."

"I remember you said that years ago when you first interviewed me."

"I'm sorry that I failed you, Cora. I really am."

Cora's big eyes softened. "It's not your fault, Jacob. I know you did everything you could."

Jacob shrugged, but the guilt wouldn't ease up.

"Once the security company shows up, I'm going to visit the nurse who was in charge of the neonatal unit when you delivered," Jacob said. "Maybe she remembered something that didn't strike her as important at the time."

"I'll go with you," Cora said.

Jacob hesitated, debating on letting her come along. Then again, he didn't want to leave her alone.

Especially in light of her ex-husband's phone call. Drew could have called last night just because he was angry.

Or...what if he'd called to see if Cora had survived the accident?

The attempt on Cora's life had come while he was questioning the Westbrooks.

But Drew could have hired someone to kill Cora just as he could have Philips.

CORA QUICKLY SHOWERED and dressed before the security company arrived. While they installed the system, Jacob drove home for a shower and clean clothes.

As the technicians worked, Cora stood looking out her window. She usually felt safe here in the mountains, as if it was a sanctuary until she was reunited with her daughter.

Now everything had changed.

The woods looked spooky, a place for predators to hide. The mountains seemed taller, the cliffs steeper, the ridges sharper and more ominous. The river seemed colder, the rapids more intense and dangerous, as if they could carry a dead body downstream and it would be lost forever.

She gripped her hands and fought panic. She could

not think like that. She was not a defeatist. She refused to allow fear to hold her hostage.

Jacob would keep her safe. She had to hold on to the hope that they were making progress.

Jacob returned just as the installation was complete, and the security specialist demonstrated how to work the system.

A half hour later, they parked at Wynona Baker's house. Wynona, who had been kind to Cora at the hospital, had worked in the neonatal unit for fifteen years before Alice was taken.

Wynona invited them in, and they settled at her kitchen table. Ceramic puppies lined a shelf in her kitchen and a picture of a chocolate Lab hung above the fireplace in the corner.

Cora wondered if Alice had a dog.

"How are you, Cora?" Wynona asked.

Cora and Jacob exchanged a look, then Cora murmured that she was okay. Jacob explained about Kurt's death and the events of the day before.

"Oh my goodness," Wynona said. "I'm so sorry, Cora. I hoped you were stopping by with good news."

"I wish we were," Cora said.

"Wynona, it's been five years," Jacob said calmly. "Sometimes immediately following a trauma, our memory is foggy because we're in shock. Have you recalled anything about that night since? Some detail about what happened in the hospital nursery?"

Wynona rubbed her fingers together in a nervous gesture. "I just remember how awful it was. The minute the fire alarm rang and we realized it was real, not a drill, everyone sprang into action. I ordered staff to move the babies out."

"There's some question now as to whether Cora's daughter was taken when the babies were outside on the lawn or before," Jacob said.

Cora scrunched her face in thought. Did Jacob know something he hadn't told her?

JACOB HAD QUESTIONED the entire staff who worked on the maternity floor after the fire, but at the time, no one had stuck out as suspicious. Most everyone's story matched—it was pure chaos, everyone was scurrying around trying to help patients evacuate and calm family members. A couple of infants had been snatched from their bassinets by parents who were close by the nursery when the fire alarm sounded.

No one had seen anyone take Cora's child.

Jacob consulted the notes from his interviews with the staff. "I talked to Dale Friedman and Horace Whitman, two of the orderlies you said helped move the infants. Was there anything odd about either one of them? Maybe a family member who'd lost a child?"

Wynona rubbed her forehead. "Not that I recall. Both Dale and Horace were hard workers. Dale went on to medical school and is doing a residency in the ER in Atlanta now. Horace became a med tech."

Cora shifted. "Please think," she said. "Did you notice anyone lurking around the nursery who didn't belong?"

Wynona sighed, the sound filled with frustration. "I'm sorry, Cora, I…just can't remember."

"My husband left my room before the alarm went off," Cora said. "Did you see him in the hall or by the nursery?"

Wynona rubbed her temple. "I saw him by the vending machine getting coffee. He was talking to a young woman. She had flowers and a baby gift with her. A little pink teddy bear, I think it was."

Jacob chewed the inside of his cheek. Wynona hadn't mentioned this before. "Do you know who the woman was?"

The nurse shook her head no. "She gave him a hug and congratulated him on the baby. They started down the hall toward the nursery, and I assumed he was going to show her your daughter, but the woman's phone rang, and she disappeared down the hall."

"What happened after that?" Jacob asked.

"I don't know. The alarm sounded, and everyone went into a panic."

Jacob retrieved a photo of Drew and his wife on his phone and showed it to Wynona. "Was this the woman you saw talking to Drew?"

Wynona studied the picture for a minute, then nodded. "Yes, I believe it was."

"That's Drew's wife," Cora said tightly. "She worked for his law firm at the time."

Jacob considered the information. If Drew had been having an affair, was it with Hilary? That would explain how quickly they'd married after his divorce.

"There's something else I'd like for you to look at," Jacob told Wynona. On his last stop to Liam's office, he'd copied footage of the person in scrubs carrying the bundle toward the laundry area.

He angled the phone for Wynona and Cora to see. A pained silence fell across the room as they watched the footage.

"Do you have any idea who that person could be?" Jacob asked.

Emotions clouded Wynona's face. "No. I can't see his—or her—face."

He had another clip of the activity on the maternity wing. "Look at this and see if anything strikes you as off."

A frown puckered the skin between Wynona's eyes. "Wait," she said, her breath catching. "That woman there, the one in the dark coat."

Cora leaned forward, anxious. Jacob gave Wynona another minute.

"What is it?" he asked.

"Her name is Evie Hanson. I don't know why she was there. She was put on suspension two weeks before the fire."

"Why was she placed on suspension?"

Wynona bit down on her lower lip. "I hate to gossip."

"Please," Cora said again. "What happened?"

"She learned she couldn't have children," Wynona said. "She was really depressed about it. One of the doctors found her sneaking into the nursery to hold the newborns."

Jacob clenched his jaw. Why hadn't this come up before? "Where is she now?"

"I don't know," Wynona said. "I thought she moved away before the fire."

"We have to find her," Cora said. "What if she was so depressed that she kidnapped Alice?"

Chapter Twelve

"Why didn't you tell us about her before?" Cora fought to keep anger from her voice, but it broke through anyway.

Jacob touched Cora's arm, a silent message to remain calm. She knotted her hands, though, and squared her shoulders. She'd been patronized and treated like she was unstable so many times that her defenses rose.

Wynona looked taken back. "I'm sorry, I didn't think about it. I thought she was gone. I hadn't seen her in the hospital in days."

"And looking at the photograph triggered your memory," Jacob said gently.

Wynona nodded, her lip quivering. "If I'd seen her and thought she might be involved, I would have come to you, Sheriff." She turned to Cora. "Not a day has gone by that I haven't regretted what happened that night. I'd been a nurse for fifteen years before that horrible fire. Although we'd lost a baby or two due to health issues, no child had ever been stolen from our nursery. When I first came on board, I instigated stringent security measures to prevent a possible kidnapping and baby mix-up."

A tense second passed.

"Did you know Evie?" Cora asked.

Wynona offered her a small smile. "I did. And it's not what you think, Cora. Evie was sweet and giving, and she loved children. She worked in the pediatric heart unit."

Questions nagged at Cora but compassion also surfaced. "She must have been devastated to learn she couldn't have children."

"She was," Wynona said. "The counselor on staff assured Evie she was a good candidate for adoption. So I don't see any reason she'd do something as drastic as to kidnap your baby."

Cora wanted to believe her. From Wynona's comments, Evie sounded like a wonderful person. If she had taken Alice, at least her little girl was in loving hands.

"That may be true," Jacob said. "But I need to question her. Do you have any idea where she is?"

Wynona shook her head. "I really don't know. So many people left Whistler after the fire that I lost track. You know it took months to rebuild the wings of the hospital that were damaged and employees were transferred to other hospitals."

Cora clung to the hope that Evie might have answers for them. Or that she might actually have Alice.

Her heart pounded with anticipation at the thought.

JACOB'S PHONE BUZZED with a text as he and Cora left Wynona's house. "Liam is going to meet us at the police station."

"Does he have information?"

"He didn't say. But I want him to find Evie Hanson."

"So do I." Hope flashed in Cora's eyes. "I wish Wynona had mentioned Evie five years ago."

Jacob ground his teeth. "That would have been help-ful."

He offered Cora a sympathetic smile, then veered onto Main Street toward his office. "Do you want me to drop you at home before I meet with Liam?"

"No, I want to know if he can find Evie."

Jacob felt the sudden need to protect her from false hope. "She might not have Alice," Jacob reminded her.

Her lips curled downward into a frown. "I know. And don't worry about me, I've survived disappoint-ment before."

Cora leaned toward the window, and he realized she was watching a woman and little girl enter the book-store. The longing on her face twisted at his heart-strings.

He passed the store, then pulled into the space desig-nated for the sheriff. Cora was out of the car before he could go around to open her door. A lot of young men these days didn't bother, but his father had taught him and his brothers to be gentlemen.

A breeze stirred the air, the temperature in the high seventies. The sun had fought through the clouds from the night before. With the summer break, the park across from the sheriff's department was full. The town seemed crowded, with vacationers flocking to the mountains for hiking, white water rafting and camping. The Whistler B & B had three cars in front, a good sign.

The owner, Beula Mayberry, had been struggling lately, but he'd heard she'd renovated, so hopefully busi-ness would pick up.

He spoke to his deputy as he entered, but he was talking on the phone, so Jacob escorted Cora to his of-fice. "Do you want coffee?" he asked.

"No, thanks." She paused and looked around the interior, focusing on the bulletin board above his desk, where he'd tacked two fliers for wanted felons along with a missing persons flier for a teenager who'd disappeared from Raleigh three weeks before.

Liam rapped his knuckles on the door and poked his head inside. Jacob waved him in and gestured toward Cora.

Liam offered his hand. "We met before, Cora."

"I remember," Cora said. "Jacob said you were still searching for my daughter. I appreciate it."

"We never gave up," Liam assured her. "Unfortunately leads went cold for a while, but that could change." He paused, then cleared his throat. "As a matter of fact, one of the major news stations is running a special segment to showcase missing persons' and children's cases that have gone cold. They do it every so often. Sometimes people recognize the child from our photographs, or recall details they've forgotten, and we get a lead."

Cora drummed her fingers on her arm. "They're going to include Alice?"

Liam nodded. "I insisted. I've already sent over the information we have on her disappearance along with your sketches."

Cora blinked as if fighting tears, and Jacob wanted to hug his brother.

He shared his conversation with the nurse. "We need to locate Evie Hanson and question her."

Liam gave a quick nod. "I'll text my analyst and have her start searching." He quickly sent a text, then gestured to Jacob's desk. "I have some photographs I'd like you to look at, Cora."

Liam set a folder on the table, then removed a photograph of a thin dark-haired woman wearing a gray suit. Her expression was drawn and sad.

"Her name is Lydia Bainbridge," Liam said. "She and her husband lived in Chapel Hill and lost a baby when it was born. A heart defect."

"That's awful," Cora murmured.

"It was and they didn't take it very well," Liam said.

"When did this happen?" Jacob asked.

"Three weeks before Cora delivered," Liam replied.

"The timing could be significant," Jacob added.

"Yes. The husband sued the doctor for incompetence, and they settled out of court. After that, they moved to Florida. They adopted a little girl two weeks after Alice went missing. One of our agents is investigating the adoption now."

"You think they may have adopted Alice?" Cora asked.

Liam shrugged. "I don't know, but we're exploring every possibility." He angled the photograph toward Cora, then added another picture of the husband, a tall auburn-haired man in a fire fighter's uniform.

Jacob and Liam exchanged a silent message. If the husband wanted to set a fire, he'd know how to do it and get away with it.

Liam tapped the photograph. "Look at this picture, Cora. Do you recall seeing this woman or man at the hospital when you were there?"

CORA SCRUTINIZED THE picture of the couple.

"I'm sorry, but I don't recall seeing them. They could have been there, but I was already in labor when I was admitted, so I was wheeled to a labor and delivery room. I stayed there for hours until the birth."

"You didn't go into the hall to walk?" Jacob asked.

She pinched the bridge of her nose. "No." Frustration knotted her insides. "I was so exhausted I fell asleep shortly after the birth. When the alarm sounded, all I could think about was saving Alice."

"I know it was mass confusion," Jacob said. He'd been there.

Liam patted Cora's hand. "It's all right. It was a long shot. They may not have been there. But my analyst is reviewing every inch of the security footage." Liam slid another folder beneath the one of the couple. "We're also working another angle." He glanced at Jacob as if uncertain whether he should continue.

"Please tell me," Cora said. "I promise I won't break down and go maniacal on you."

Jacob chuckled, and so did Liam. "I'm not worried about that," Liam said. "And if you did, I'd understand. Missing children bring out emotions in all of us."

Cora swallowed back a sob. Compassion and tenderness triggered tears every time.

"What's in the other file?" Jacob asked.

Liam scrubbed a hand through his hair, then removed a photograph of a middle-aged lady with graying hair. She was seated on a train with a baby boy and a toddler girl. "An agent in Atlanta sent me a picture of this woman. She goes by the name Deidre Coleman." Liam paused. "We believe she's running an illegal adoption ring."

Cora made a pained sound.

"One of our agents is going undercover to verify our suspicions," Liam said. "At this point, we've uncovered reports of three missing children, including that baby boy, who match photographs of recently adopted children on the dark web and linked them back to her. So far, no legal documents have been located. But we traced large sums of money deposited into an offshore account in the name of Deidre Coleman, although we believe that name is an alias. Our agent is gathering intel for a warrant to pick her up for questioning."

He angled his head toward Cora. "Do you ever remember seeing this woman? It could have been at the hospital or around town or even at your ob-gyn's office."

Cora studied every detail of the woman's face. Although she was definitely in the shadows in the picture, she could tell the woman was austere. A blunt nose. Graying, thin eyebrows. Long fingers with nails that needed a manicure. Even though she was seated, she held a firm grip on the toddler's hand and cradled the baby close to her, its face hidden.

Cora closed her eyes, mentally transporting herself back to her ob-gyn's office. So many happy, pregnant women congregating to share stories and the excitement of upcoming births. Talk of nurseries, baby showers, and little girl and boy names. Laughter over arguments between spouses and grandparents over those names. Talk of different parenting styles.

Dreams of finally nestling their baby in their arms.

Occasionally a woman leaving teary-eyed over bad news. But this woman in the picture—*she* would have stood out in the maternity waiting room because she'd passed her childbearing years.

"I don't remember seeing her at my doctor's office," Cora said. "I guess she could have come in the hospital, or maybe she was on the lawn that night." She gave

Liam a pointed look. "Have you found a link between her and Alice?"

Regret darkened Liam's face. "Not yet, but we're looking."

Disappointment threatened to steal her budding hope, but she squashed it. With both Jacob and Liam on her side now, at least Alice hadn't been forgotten.

"I'll keep you posted, Cora." Liam gathered the photographs and files and Cora thanked him.

"Let me know if you locate Evie Hanson," Jacob said.

Liam agreed, said goodbye and headed outside.

Jacob stood and adjusted his belt where his gun hung, drawing her gaze to his big, strong body.

Cora jerked her eyes away. How could she possibly think about how handsome Jacob was when they'd just been discussing an illegal adoption ring?

When the woman with the graying hair might be stealing babies and selling them.

When Jacob had told his brother he wasn't interested in her personally.

Chapter Thirteen

The thought of a person selling children nauseated Cora.

"You want me to drive you home now or to pick up a rental car?" Jacob asked.

She shook her head. "I'll take care of it." Waiting alone at home did not appeal to her at the moment. She was afraid she'd get mired in the fact that she had endless days ahead with nothing to do but think about her daughter and her jobless future.

She brushed her hands down her shirt as she stood. "I'm going to the bookstore for a while."

"All right. Call me if you need anything," Jacob offered.

She thanked him and slipped from his office, determined to keep her feelings for him at bay.

A dark cloud had formed, shrouding the sun and adding a chill to the air as Cora walked down the sidewalk and crossed the street to the bookstore. Mothers and children filled the park, their laughter and chatter a reminder that life moved on, that happiness did exist.

Even if it evaded her.

One day she'd push Alice in the swings and fly a kite with her, and they'd skate on the rink the town erected for the winter holidays.

She reached the bookstore and smiled at the array of children's books displayed for the summer reading program. Through the glass window, she saw Nina at one of the tables drawing, with Faye close by. A minute later, Faye opened her laptop and Cora noticed her browsing the real estate website where she worked.

Envy stirred inside Cora. If she found Alice, would they ever be that close?

She desperately wanted to join them, but Faye's shared confidence gave her pause. The poor woman had suffered.

She didn't intend to add to her problems.

Clutching her purse, she walked toward the diner. Inside, the place was bustling with the late-afternoon lunch crowd. She slipped up to the bar, ordered a turkey sandwich and sweet tea, then phoned to arrange a rental car as she waited on her meal.

The owner, a cheery lady named Billie Jean, grinned at her. "There you go, sweetie. You doing okay today?"

"Sure." Cora forced a smile. Discussing baby kidnapping rings wasn't her idea of fun, but if it helped find Alice or saved another mother from experiencing the pain she'd suffered, she'd look at any pictures Liam or Jacob showed her.

She paid for the sandwich and drink, carried them across the street to the park and found an empty picnic table beneath a live oak. The shade of the tree offered her privacy, but also allowed her to people-watch.

Signs for a watermelon festival in two weeks had been tacked up around the park along with a sign for Pet Adoption Day the following Saturday. She'd considered adopting a dog over the years to keep her company, but wanted to wait until Alice came home so they could choose the pet together.

She spread out her sketchbook and pencils on the table, and nibbled on her sandwich as she studied the children on the playground. A little curly-haired blond toddler in a purple romper was learning to walk and kept stumbling. The mother clapped and laughed, offering encouragement as she called the child's name.

A group of elementary-aged children played chase while a father tossed the ball to his son in a game of catch.

She was just about to begin a new sketch of Alice when the sound of a woman's voice made her pulse clamor.

"Cora?"

She clenched her pencil as she faced the woman. Julie Batton. At one time, they'd been best friends.

Before Alice had been taken.

Julie's little boy, Brian, looked up at her with the same grass-green eyes as his mother. Cora remembered the day he was born as if it was yesterday.

It had been exactly one week before Alice came into the world.

Cora had cooked Julie and her husband dinner that night and carried the excited couple a bottle of champagne. They'd toasted the occasion and laughed over dreams they shared for their children.

Cora's homecoming had been the opposite. Filled with fear and anguish. Police hovering around, asking questions. People staring at her and Drew with sympathy and suspicion.

Julie had tried to be a friend. She'd sent cookies. Offered Cora a shoulder to cry on.

But the day Cora followed a woman with a stroller in the mall, Julie had told Cora she needed psychiatric help.

Then she'd run to Drew. Made it seem like Cora was losing her mind. Drew had gotten rid of Alice's things later because of the counselor—and Julie.

She'd never forgiven either one of them for that.

FIVE MINUTES AFTER Cora left, Jacob's phone buzzed. Liam.

"My analyst just called. They located Evie Hanson. She's been working at a hospital about twenty miles from Whistler." Liam paused. "I have a conference call with the task force investigating the baby kidnapping/adoption ring. I'm texting you Evie's home address so you can check it out. According to our information, Evie took a leave of absence about three months ago to be a stay-at-home mom."

"Is that timing significant?" Jacob asked.

Liam hissed out a breath. "Could be, could be co-incidental."

"What does that mean?"

"Means it warrants further investigation."

Jacob snatched his keys, anxious to leave. "I'm on my way to question her."

"Jacob, listen, man," Liam said in a no-nonsense voice. "It's possible she may not be involved in the Reeves-Westbrook baby kidnapping. Even if she obtained the baby through the ring, she may be unaware that the child was kidnapped, so tread carefully. If you suspect at any point that she bought the baby, play it cool and don't reveal our suspicions. We don't want to spook her into running or into alerting Deidre Coleman that we're on to her."

"You got it."

Jacob met Martin on the way out the door, relayed the latest turn of events and asked him to cover rounds.

His senses were alert for trouble as he drove through town. This afternoon looked like a normal day in Whistler.

So had the day of the fire, when everything had gone horribly wrong. No one in town had seen it coming. No one knew why the fire was set and the town destroyed.

He passed the square, and veered onto the road leading from town, his adrenaline having spiked at the prospect of solving this case. He sped up once he left the city limits, then maneuvered the curvy roads toward Shady Oak.

The nurse lived in a development a mile from the village of Shady Oak, a quaint little town built in the valley between the mountains.

Minutes later, he reached her house. It was a sprawling ranch house with green shutters and a well-maintained lawn. He scanned the yard and property for a car or children's toys, any sign indicating the family was home.

He parked in the drive, then climbed out and walked up to the door. The carport was empty, no cars in sight.

He rang the doorbell, but when no one answered, he peeked into the windows flanking the front door.

He didn't see movement or anyone inside. He gritted his teeth.

Had Evie left town because she knew the feds were on their tail?

"Cora, is it okay if I sit with you for a minute?" Julie asked.

Cora inhaled to calm her voice. The last thing she

needed was to make a scene. Besides, maybe Julie had been right five years ago. She had been out of control.

"Of course." Cora gestured toward the bench seat across from her and Julie slid onto it, angling her body to keep an eye on Brian as he played with another boy about his age. They were tossing a football back and forth. Brian dropped it and giggled, then growled like a monster. Cora couldn't contain a smile.

"Brian has really grown," Cora said. "Was he in kindergarten this year?"

"He was," Julie said. "That's his friend Tony. He lives a couple doors down from us."

"Cute boys," she said. "I'm sure he keeps you busy."

Julie smiled as she watched her son. "He's all boy, that's for sure. Loves cars and trucks, sports and superheroes. He dressed as Spider-Man last year for Halloween."

"Superheroes were the theme this year at school," Cora said with a pang of sadness that she'd miss the school activities next year.

An awkward silence fell between them for a minute. Julie took a sip from her water bottle, then offered Cora a tender look that reminded Cora of when they were good friends. Julie had always worn her feelings on her sleeve. She volunteered at the women's shelter, prepared meals for the homeless, and ran the clothing and food drive at her church.

Julie was one of the most selfless people she'd ever known. They'd actually met during one of the food drives one year and bonded as they sorted and packed canned goods for families who'd lost their homes in a tornado.

"I've been thinking about you a lot," Julie said. "I

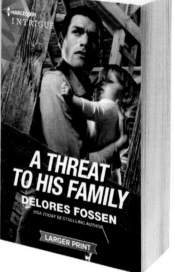

Get 2
FREE FABULOUS BOOKS
You Love!

To thank you for being a loyal reader we'd like to send you 2 FREE BOOKS, absolutely free.

Just write "YES" on the Loyal Reader Voucher and we'll send you 2 Free Books and 2 Free Mystery Gifts, altogether worth over $20, as a way of saying thank you for being a loyal reader.

We are so glad you love the books as much as we do and can't wait to send you great new books.

So don't miss out, return your Loyal Reader Voucher Today!

Pam Powers

LOYAL READER
FREE BOOKS VOUCHER

YES! I Love Reading, please send me 2 FREE BOOKS and 2 FREE Mystery Gifts.

Just write in "YES" on the dotted line below then return this card today and we'll send your free books & gifts asap!

➡️ _ YES _ ⬅️

Which do you prefer?

☐ **I prefer Regular-Print**
182/382 HDL GNS4

☐ **I prefer Larger-Print**
199/399 HDL GNS4

FIRST NAME	LAST NAME

ADDRESS

APT.#	CITY

STATE/PROV.   ZIP/POSTAL CODE

HI-220-OMLR20

wanted to see you, but I didn't know if you'd want to see me."

"I'm sorry you felt that way," Cora said. "I was rough on you after Alice was taken." Cora breathed out. It felt good—right—to apologize and let go of her anger. "No matter what happened, though, I was happy for you, and glad you had Brian. I never meant to imply that I wasn't."

Tears flooded Julie's eyes. "I know that," she said. "I always did. And it wasn't your fault. My God, Cora, you're stronger than I am. I don't think I could have gone on if I was in your shoes."

Cora made a low sound in her throat. "Truthfully, Julie, I'm still a wreck. But I'm trying not to give up hope."

Julie reached across the table, and Cora linked hands with her the way they used to do. "I'm so sorry I wasn't there for you the way you needed." Julie wiped at a tear with her free hand. "I just didn't know what to do, Cora. I felt so bad for you, and I was terrified at the same time. I was a mess myself over not being able to conceive."

Cora raised her brows. "What? I'm sorry. I didn't know."

"Because I didn't want anyone to know," Julie admitted quietly. "I was…ashamed. I felt like a failure when we kept trying to get pregnant and couldn't."

Cora's heart broke for her friend. "Oh, gosh, Julie, there was nothing to be ashamed of. A lot of women have trouble conceiving."

"I know that up here." She tapped her forehead, then her chest. "But my heart said something else. I felt like I wasn't a good wife, that I was letting Jimmy down." She swallowed hard. "Anyway, that's the reason I pulled back from you. I kept thinking, what if it was Brian? What if someone took my little boy?" Julie choked on the last word, emotions overcoming her.

Cora squeezed Julie's hand. She'd been so wrapped up in her own pain and terror that she hadn't considered anyone's feelings but her own. "I guess that's the reason you reacted so strongly when I chased down that woman at the mall."

Julie started to say something, but Cora threw up a warning hand. "I'm not making excuses for it. It was wrong. I'm sure I terrified that poor lady. I understand now why you told Drew."

Julie's brows wrinkled. "I didn't tell Drew about that day."

Cora narrowed her eyes. "You didn't?"

Julie shook her head no. "I went home and cried and rocked Brian for hours. I felt so sorry for you. I wanted to make it up to you, but I didn't know how."

"If you didn't tell Drew, how did he find out?" Cora asked.

"I have no idea. The only person I told was Jimmy."

"Do you think he called Drew and told him?"

"No, I made him promise not to," Julie admitted. "Besides, he was too worried about me. I hadn't been sleeping and was falling apart at home. He insisted I talk to a therapist the next day, and I did."

"You went to therapy?"

Julie nodded. "I should have gone when we first couldn't conceive. The counselor helped me understand my feelings and learn to control my anxiety about the possibility of losing Brian."

"Oh, Julie, I'm so sorry," Cora said. "I should have been there for you."

"No, you were looking for your baby," Julie said brokenly. "There's no one to blame, Cora. It was just a horrible situation."

And Drew had made it worse for Cora by giving all of her baby things away.

The question still nagged at her, though. If Julie hadn't told Drew about the incident at the mall, how had he known?

Chapter Fourteen

Jacob moved from window to window, looking inside Evie Hanson's house.

She was gone.

On the off chance she'd left something, *anything* behind, even a scrap of paper with a forwarding address, he walked around to the back of the house and checked the door. Locked. On the far side, he found the laundry room window ajar, so he climbed through it.

A washer and dryer remained. He peeked inside the dryer and found a lone little pink sock.

His heart twisted.

A child's sock, a little girl probably about the same age as Alice.

He stuck it in his pocket and moved from the laundry room into the hallway, then the kitchen. He scanned the room and searched the drawers. Cleaned out, as well.

Dammit.

He searched the living room next, combed through the coat closet and desk. He glanced inside and found it empty, then ran his hand along the top shelf. Nothing but dust.

Frustrated, he strode down the hallway to the first

bedroom. A bed and dresser, but nothing inside the chest or closet, either.

The bathroom yielded a couple of bandages with cartoon imprints, a nail file and a little pink toothbrush. His instincts kicked in, and he removed a baggie from inside his pocket and bagged the toothbrush for DNA analysis.

If it matched Alice's, he'd ask the crime scene techs to search for prints. He also needed to research Evie's banking information, find out if she rented or owned, and if she'd left a forwarding address.

He moved to the smaller bedroom. The twin bed suggested it belonged to the child. Marks from where posters and pictures had been removed discolored the lavender walls. Bare shelves in the closet, although some digging unearthed a book caught in a corner. It was a children's book about giving a mouse a cookie. The soft cover was tattered, the pages worn, the book obviously well-loved.

He bagged the book then skimmed his hand along the top of the shelf. His hand brushed something in the back, and he stretched his hand and snagged the item. A small notebook.

He opened it and found pictures the child had drawn.

One picture stood out. It was a Christmas tree with a string of colorful lights.

Cora liked to draw. Could this child be Alice?

JULIE GESTURED TOWARD Cora's sketchbook. "I see you're still drawing," Julie said. "Working on anything in particular?"

Cora closed her journal. If she was going to be

friends with Julie again, she had to be honest. Sane but honest.

"It may sound strange, but I've sketched images of what I think Alice would look like over the years."

Worry flashed across Julie's face, then a gentle smile. "You must think about her every day." She reached for the sketchbook. "Can I take a look?"

Cora shrugged. "Actually I'm just starting a new series. I…gave some of the sketches to the sheriff to send to the FBI. They're going to distribute to law enforcement agencies and NCMEC."

"It's great that you can do something to help," Julie said.

"I don't know if it will," Cora admitted. "I wonder how much Alice has changed. If I'd even recognize her."

A sad look passed across Julie's face. "I have a feeling you will."

Cora's gaze met hers, her compassion a reminder of Julie's confession about her own anxiety.

"Well, we'll see. The FBI is coordinating with a special news segment about missing persons' and children's cases. I'm hoping someone will recognize her and come forward."

Julie squeezed her hand again. "I'll pray that happens, Cora."

They held hands for a moment, the anger and bitterness that had driven them apart slipping away. After the last few lonely years, it was comforting to have a female friend. Someone who wasn't a shrink.

Brian ran over, his cheeks red from playing. "Mommy, can we get ice cream now?"

Julie smiled and ruffled her son's hair. "Of course." She turned to Cora. "Would you like to go with us?"

Cora hesitated, but decided it was time she started behaving like a friend. Maybe having Julie back in her life would help ease the loneliness of the summer.

And waylay the feelings she had for Jacob.

She would just have to keep her obsession with staring at every little girl for her daughter's face under control.

She gathered her things and walked beside Julie as they crossed the park to the street, then the ice cream store. The boys' excitement was contagious. As soon as they entered the ice cream parlor, Brian and his friend Tony started counting the different flavors.

It took twenty minutes for them to decide while she and Julie chose their favorite, mint chocolate chip, a common love they'd discovered the first time they met. They sat at a small table outside and the kids licked their cones, the summer breeze stirring the scent of flowers and an impending rain shower.

Down the street at the bookstore, she saw Faye and Nina exiting, Nina chattering and holding hands with her mother. Cora's heart swelled with longing, but she forced herself to turn away.

The boys finished their cones, and Julie handed them napkins to clean their faces. "Guess we'd better go," Julie said. "I have to get Brian's friend home." She paused as she stood. "What are you doing?"

Cora offered a smile, her brows knitting as a few raindrops began to fall. "I need to pick up a rental car."

"I can give you a lift if you want," Julie offered.

Cora tossed her trash into the bin. "I'd appreciate that."

Together they walked to Julie's minivan and climbed in. "Where are you living now?"

"The cottage Drew and I bought. After we split, I moved in permanently."

Julie gave her a sympathetic look. "I'm sorry about your divorce, Cora. That must have been difficult."

Cora lifted her chin. "I'm fine now."

"I can't believe Hilary and Drew ended up together." Julie's voice softened. "I want you to know that I stopped hanging out with her after they got married. It just…didn't seem right."

"I'm sorry you were caught in the middle." Cora meant it, too.

Julie's comment triggered the memory of Jacob's question. She'd been shocked when she'd realized Drew and Hilary were getting close.

Hilary had stopped by personally to tell her about their engagement. She claimed she felt bad, but that Drew was hurting over Alice's disappearance, too. That she'd tried to be there for Cora, but Cora had pushed her away.

While consoling Drew, they'd fallen in love.

Maybe the divorce had been her fault. In her anguish, she'd pushed him right into Hilary's arms.

JACOB FLIPPED THE pages of the drawing pad and discovered other childlike pictures, then one of a baby crib that was empty. Curiosity filled him, but he couldn't make too much out of the drawings. They could mean nothing.

Still, he'd send them to the lab with everything else.

He finished searching the closet, but found nothing else, then walked back through the house. "Where are you, Evie? Do you have Cora's daughter?"

He left through the back door, scanned the property

and noted a neighbor's car next door. The houses were situated on small lots with shrubbery in between.

The houses directly across the street looked vacant, but the green sedan in the drive of the ranch next door indicated someone was home. He hurried up the drive, noting the wreath of spring flowers on the door and the bird feeder in the front yard. A swing set sat in the backyard, visible from the front stoop, and a soccer goal occupied the corner by the fence.

Jacob knocked on the door, tapping his foot as he waited. A minute later, the door swung open, and a boy about ten grinned at him with mud on his face. Jacob couldn't help but smile. The boy reminded him of mud fights and makeshift obstacle courses with his brothers in the backyard when he was that age.

"Hey," the boy said with a toothy grin.

Jacob smiled back. "Is your mother or your father here?"

"Ridley, what are you doing?" A woman's voice screeched. "I told you not to open the door to strangers."

A thirtysomething woman appeared in jeans and a T-shirt, wiping her hands on a dish towel, something that looked like chocolate frosting on her face. Maybe it was frosting on the kid's face, too.

"But Mama, he's a cop," Ridley said. "I seen his police car out the window."

"You saw it, not seen it," his mother corrected. She turned her attention to Jacob. "Sheriff?"

"Yes, Sheriff Maverick. I'd like to ask you a couple of questions."

She patted her son's shoulder. "Ridley, Inez needs some playtime. Why don't you take her out back and throw the tennis ball with her?"

"But Mama," Ridley said. "He's the *sheriff*." His eyes grew big with interest.

His mother smiled. "I know, and I promise to tell you if something is interesting, but please take Inez out before she has an accident on the carpet."

"All right," Ridley said, glum faced.

Jacob winked at the boy. "If I need you, buddy, I'll find you outside. Okay?"

Ridley bounced up and down on the balls of his feet. "'Kay." Then he ran toward the back room calling the dog's name.

The mother escorted Jacob to the kitchen, where she could keep an eye on her son and the dog. Outside, the scruffy mutt ran in circles as she chased the tennis ball Ridley tossed to her.

"So," the woman said as she seated herself at the pine table. "What can I do for you, Sheriff?"

"Mrs….?"

"Owens," she said. "Dayna. My husband owns the hardware store up the way."

"Right. Well, I'll get to the point. Did you know the woman who lived next door?"

She nodded, but a frown creased her brows. "I met Evie a few times in passing, but we didn't really visit much. She kept to herself."

"And her daughter? What was her name?"

"Twyla," Dayna said. "She was adorable. Five, and full of energy and creativity. That child loved to draw and sing. Occasionally she and Ridley played outside together, but Evie seemed nervous and protective. Why are you asking about Evie, Sheriff? Did something happen to her?"

Jacob gave a small shrug. "I don't know. I wanted to talk to her about a connection she may have had to the hospital in Whistler five years ago, but it appears she moved out."

Dayna leaned forward and rested her elbows on the table. "That was odd."

"Where was the little girl's father?" Jacob asked.

Dayna shrugged. "It was just Evie. Her husband died in a helicopter crash in Afghanistan three years ago."

"I'm sorry." Jacob swallowed. "Did she appear to be upset about anything lately? Or did Twyla?"

"No, but like I said, they kept to themselves. I did see a delivery truck bringing in a baby crib one day about a month ago. Last week, when I asked Evie about it, she said she'd hoped to get a little boy, but it didn't work out."

Jacob narrowed his eyes. "She hoped to get a little boy?"

"Yes, they adopted Twyla. Evie was going to adopt again. I don't know what happened but she moved the next day."

She stretched to see Ridley in the yard and seemed relieved to see him climbing the jungle gym while the dog plopped down beside him and chewed on a stick.

"What day was that?"

"Saturday. That morning I saw her packing her things in her car. I went over to inquire, but she waved and took off as if she was in a hurry. I thought something was wrong but didn't get to ask."

Jacob chewed the inside of his cheek. Saturday.

Dammit. That was the day after Kurt Philips had been murdered.

CORA THANKED JULIE as she dropped her at the rental car company, and they agreed to get together later in the week.

A few raindrops splattered the ground as she drove home, so she parked quickly and hurried up the steps. She paused as she fished out her keys.

A gift basket with a bright purple bow sat in front of the doorway.

She stooped to pick it up and read the card.

A friendship offering from Whistler Mountain Realty. Faye.

It felt as if a ray of sunshine had splintered through the dark cloud hanging over her. First Julie and now Faye.

Hope sprouted that her world was about to turn around and get brighter. If it wasn't raining, she might start that garden today, but she'd wait till tomorrow for the rain to pass.

She unlocked the door and carried the basket inside. A chill invaded her, and she made a cup of coffee, then laid her sketchpad on the table in front of the window overlooking the mountains.

Then she turned to examine the items in the gift basket. A lavender-scented candle and lavender-scented bath soaps. A box of chocolates. An assortment of brownies and cookies in a tin.

Yum, she was a chocoholic.

Deciding the brownie would be perfect with her coffee, she removed one from the tin and set it on the table with a mug of coffee. She settled down in front of the window and opened her sketchpad, then began another sketch. This one of Alice eating an ice cream cone.

Only she had no idea what her daughter's favorite flavor was.

Stewing over the possibilities, she sketched the ice cream parlor with the dozens of choices, nibbling on the brownie as she drew.

Suddenly, though, her throat thickened. She coughed, gagging for a breath. She tried to sip the coffee to wash the brownie down but choked, and coffee spewed from her mouth.

She clutched her throat, desperate for air. God. She was having an allergic reaction. There must have been peanut oil in the brownie.

Her head felt light, the room swimming. She pushed away from the table and staggered toward her purse. Her EpiPen was inside.

One shot and she'd be fine.

Only the room twirled. She gasped. Her purse was just out of reach, her fingers clawing for it as darkness swept her into its abyss.

Chapter Fifteen

Cora struggled to keep her eyes open. She had to keep breathing. Reach her EpiPen. But her throat had closed…

Suddenly her door flew open. "Cora?"

Faye?

Had she forgotten to lock the door when she'd come inside? Hadn't she set the alarm…

No…she'd been distracted by the gift basket.

Footsteps clattered. Voices echoed as if far away in a tunnel.

Fear seized Cora. She didn't want to die. Then she might never find her little girl.

"Ms. Reeves?"

A small voice this time. A little girl's. Nina's?

More footsteps, then a hand gently touched her. "Ms. Reeves?"

"Cora, what's wrong?" Faye's voice this time.

Cora blinked back tears, struggling to see through the fuzziness clouding her brain. She wheezed out a breath, cried out, stretched her fingers toward the end table where she'd left her purse. "Pen…" she choked out.

"Pen?" Faye stroked Cora's hair away from her face and turned her head to examine her. "Cora, I'll call 911."

She shook her head, or at least she thought she did, then clasped her throat with one hand and pointed to her purse with the other. "Help."

Another sound. Footsteps. Smaller this time. "Mama!"

"Get me my phone!" Faye shouted.

"But Mama, look," Nina cried.

Through the fog, Cora saw Nina running toward them, the EpiPen in her small hand. "Look."

Faye's eyes widened, and she grabbed the EpiPen from Nina, then brushed Cora's cheek. "You need this?"

Cora struggled to nod, but the darkness was pulling her under.

Faye jerked the top off the pen, raised it and quickly jabbed it into Cora's thigh.

Nina cradled Cora's hand in hers. "Is she gonna be all right?" Nina whispered.

Faye soothed Cora by rubbing her hand along Cora's back. "Come on, breathe, Cora. You're going to be fine."

Slowly the ache in her chest receded. Her throat felt as if it was contracting, the swelling lessening. Perspiration trickled down her face as she clutched Faye's hand.

"Mama?"

Nina sounded frightened. Cora had to assuage the little girl's fears. She blinked, inhaling and exhaling slowly to steady her breathing. Finally the dizziness faded. The world stopped moving. Slipped back into focus.

She stared into Faye's eyes, then Nina's. Both looked frightened.

"I'll get an ambulance," Faye said.

Cora shook her head. "No… I'm okay…thanks…"

Relief flooded Faye's face, then Nina leaned over and gave her a hug. "You scared me, Ms. Reeves."

"I… I'm sorry, honey," Cora whispered.

"Can you sit up?" Faye asked.

Cora wasn't sure. Her body felt weak. Languid. Her limbs heavy.

But another look at the terror on Nina's face, and she nodded.

"Come on, I'll help you." Faye slid her arm beneath Cora's shoulders and helped her to stand. Nina clutched her arm and leaned on Faye.

They helped her to the sofa and she sank onto it, leaned back and continued to breathe in and out. Footsteps again, then Faye returned with a wet washcloth and dabbed Cora's forehead with it.

The cool cloth helped to lift the fog. "Thank you, Faye. You saved my life."

A blush stained Faye's cheeks. "I'm just relieved you're okay. I didn't know you had an allergy."

"Peanuts," Cora said. "The brownies in the basket you sent must have contained peanut oil."

"I'm allergic to peanuts, too," Nina said. "I gots a pen just like you."

Cora's heart pounded. "You do?"

"Uh-huh," Nina said. "I hate that shot. Mama had to give it to me twice."

A strange sensation engulfed Cora. She and Nina shared the same food sensitivity. A coincidence, or could it mean more?

She silently chided herself. Peanut allergies were on the rise these days. For heaven's sake, the school had issued letters to parents, making the school a peanut-free zone because the allergy was so common.

A contrite expression flashed across Faye's face. "I forgot to tell one of the mothers when Nina was invited for a playdate, and she gave Nina a muffin containing peanut oil."

"It happens to everyone at some time," Cora said sympathetically. Her mind raced. "What are you doing here anyway?"

"Nina begged to stop by." Faye wrinkled her nose. "But what did you mean, about the gift basket from me?"

Cora straightened slightly and gestured toward the table. "The basket," she said. "It had your name on the card."

Faye crossed the room and examined the basket and card. A frown tugged at the corners of her eyes. "I didn't send the basket, Cora."

If Faye hadn't sent it, who had?

Someone who knew about her allergy and wanted her to die?

JACOB HANDED THE items he'd collected from Evie Hanson's house to Liam. He had broken into the house with no warrant, so it might not be admissible, but right now all he wanted was answers and a lead. And he might have just found one.

Besides, maybe he could justify probable cause. "I thought you could run these for DNA through your lab," he said. "I'm sure you can get results faster than I can through the county."

"Sure." Liam examined the bag with the pink toothbrush, the sock and drawing pad. "You think this little girl Twyla might be Alice Reeves Westbrook?"

Jacob lifted his shoulders slightly. "It's worth exploring. She is adopted. The neighbor said Evie was protective of her daughter and they kept to themselves."

"Being protective of your child is not a crime," Liam pointed out. "In this day and age, parents should be cautious."

Agreed. "But the way she suddenly packed up and moved seems suspicious. The neighbor also claimed Evie was on the verge of adopting a baby boy, but something happened. Maybe she obtained Twyla illegally and planned to do the same again, but got frightened and decided to run."

"You could be jumping to conclusions," Liam said. "But we'll follow up."

"I texted Martin to see if he can dig up more info on Evie, who she rented from, how she paid. I'd like a crime team to search for prints in the house. Maybe Evie's job in the pediatric unit is a front for kidnapping babies."

"That's a stretch," Liam said. "But considering I'm investigating an illegal kidnapping/adoption ring, it's worth considering."

A good working theory.

"Let me start a search for her." Liam clicked some keys on his computer. "And I'll handle the prints."

"Thanks." Jacob shifted. "Any more on the kidnapping/adoption ring?"

"Not yet. Hopefully soon."

Jacob's phone buzzed on his hip. He checked the caller ID. Cora.

"Let me take this. Call me if you get a lead on Evie."

He stepped into the hall and answered the phone. "Cora?"

"Jacob, I…need to talk to you."

Her voice sounded strange. Weak. Something had happened…

"What's wrong?"

"I think someone just tried to poison me," she said in a raspy whisper.

Jacob's blood ran cold. "Where are you?"

"Home."

He hurried down the hall to leave the building. "Hang on, I'll be right there."

CORA'S MIND REELED as she studied Faye. She'd settled Nina at the table to color while they talked.

Faye seemed confused, and had adamantly denied sending the basket.

"Could someone from your real estate office have ordered it on your behalf?" Cora asked.

"I don't think so," Faye said. "We typically send gifts to potential clients. You haven't talked to anyone about putting your place on the market, have you?"

Cora shook her head. "No."

Faye rubbed her temple. "I don't understand, then."

"Did you mention me to anyone?" Cora asked. "Maybe your agency is sending out feelers to find out if anyone is interested in selling?"

Faye pursed her lips. "I haven't talked about you to anyone, Cora."

Now her tone sounded defensive.

"I'm sorry for asking so many questions," Cora said, lowering her voice so Nina wouldn't hear. "But I think whoever sent this knew about my allergy and just tried to kill me."

Shock widened Faye's eyes. "What? Oh my God. You don't think I would do that?"

Cora glanced at Nina. How could she doubt Faye with her daughter in Cora's living room? When Faye had saved her life?

If she'd wanted to kill Cora, she wouldn't have brought Nina to her house to witness it.

"No, I don't," Cora said quietly.

Faye paced the room, then found two glasses in Cora's kitchen, filled them with water then brought one to Cora. Her hand shook as she sipped from the other glass and sank into the chair facing Cora.

She leaned forward, angling her face away from Nina. "Why would you think someone wants to hurt you, Cora?"

Cora debated on how much to tell Faye. But Faye had confided about her ex, so she decided to reciprocate and explained about Kurt's murder and her car crash.

"You think the same person who murdered that private investigator tried to poison you today?" Faye asked. "If he didn't share information with you, why come after you?"

"I don't know," Cora said. "Unless whoever took Alice believes I might be close to finding her."

Faye's lips parted in a surprised expression. "But trying to kill you would only draw suspicion."

"True," Cora said. "But whoever it is must be desperate."

A knock sounded at the door, jarring them both. Cora pushed forward to get up, but Faye threw up a hand. "I'll get it. You should rest."

Cora still felt a little light-headed, so she leaned back against the sofa. Jacob's voice echoed from across the room, and Faye introduced herself, then led him inside.

A muscle ticked in Jacob's jaw as his dark gaze met hers.

Faye paused beside Nina and patted her shoulder. "Come on, sweetie, we need to go."

Nina ran over and threw her arms around Cora. "Are you gonna be okay, Ms. Reeves?"

Cora hugged her tightly, savoring the sweetness of the little girl. "I'm fine, honey." She cupped Nina's face between her hands and gave her a smile. "Thanks to you and your quick thinking."

Nina's big eyes brightened. "You want us to come back and check on you?"

She did. But Faye seemed agitated and ready to go, so she didn't want to push it.

Jacob saved her from having to respond. "Don't worry, I'll make sure Ms. Reeves is okay."

"Good," Nina said with a toothy grin. "'Cause she's the bestest teacher in the world."

"I'm sorry I scared you, honey," Cora said softly. "You were very brave today, Nina."

Nina hugged her again, and Cora fought tears.

Faye set her water glass on the table beside Cora's, then clasped Nina's hand. "Come on, sweetheart. Cora needs rest."

Cora offered Faye a smile of gratitude. "Thank you so much, Faye."

Faye nodded. "I'm just glad we got here when we did."

Cora remembered seeing them in town. "Did you stop by for a reason?"

Faye gave a sheepish shrug. "We saw you leaving the park and just wanted to say hi. Call me if you need anything."

Nina waved, and she and Faye left. Seeing them and

Julie today made Cora realize how much she'd shut herself off from others.

Maybe she and Faye could be friends.

But she turned to Jacob and reality intruded. He was here because someone wanted her dead.

And today they'd almost succeeded.

Chapter Sixteen

Jacob crossed the room to Cora, anger mingling with worry. "Do you need a doctor?"

"No, I'm all right," Cora said. "Faye gave me my EpiPen."

Jacob lowered himself beside her. Her complexion looked pale, her eyes slightly glazed, and perspiration dotted her forehead. "What allergy?" he said, all business.

"Peanuts," she said. "I know what foods to avoid, but when I found the gift basket I saw the brownies and didn't think about them having peanut oil in them. But they must have. I was fine until I ate one."

He narrowed his eyes, then he seemed to scan the room for the basket.

Cora pointed toward the table. "That was on the front porch when I arrived home. The card said it was from Faye and her real estate agency, but she denies sending it."

Jacob chewed the inside of his cheek. "Did she know about your allergy?"

Cora took a sip of water. "I don't see how she could have. We only just met."

"Who knew about your allergy?" Jacob asked.

Cora ran her fingers through her hair. "Some of the teachers at school. Of course Drew and all my former friends."

He folded his arms. "Isn't Faye the woman who complained to your principal?"

Cora clenched her jaw. "She is. But we came to an understanding when she told me about her ex."

"What was she doing here?" Jacob asked in a tone full of distrust.

"She and Nina saw me in town and decided to stop by and say hi."

"Has she ever done that before?"

Cora shook her head no. "But like I said, we're just getting to know each other. I think she felt bad about having me fired."

Jacob mulled over that possibility. Faye had seemed perfectly normal. Friendly, although maybe a little wary. "She was in a hurry to leave when I came in."

"I think my reaction frightened her and Nina," Cora admitted.

"Was the child upset?" Jacob asked.

Cora's expression softened. "Actually Nina was a trouper. She grabbed the EpiPen from my purse. Her quick thinking saved my life."

Jacob pulled a hand down his chin. "How did she know about the pen?"

Cora searched her memory. The last hour was blurred. "I tried to tell them. And… Nina is allergic to peanuts, too. Maybe she recognized the signs of my reaction because she's had a similar reaction before."

Jacob retrieved his phone from his belt. He examined the gift basket, read the card, then punched the florist's number.

"This is Sheriff Jacob Maverick. I have a question about an order delivered to Cora Reeves. Can you tell me who placed the order?"

He waited while she searched their records. "Actually the order was placed online."

"The name of the sender?"

"Whistler Mountain Realty."

"Was there an individual's name?" Jacob asked.

"No, sir." .

"How was it paid for?"

"Hmm, looks like a PayPal account. Sheriff, is something wrong?"

"I don't know. Maybe." He'd need a warrant to search the accounts. Unless Liam could gain access…

"Let me know if that account orders anything again."

"I sure will."

He ended the call, then phoned the real estate agency, tapping his foot in agitation. Cora was watching him with avid curiosity.

"This is Penny from Whistler Mountain Realty," a cheery young woman answered.

Jacob identified himself and explained the reason he called. "Did someone from your agency order a gift basket for Cora Reeves?"

"Hang on, and I'll check." Jazz music echoed over the line while he was on hold. A second later, she returned. "I'm sorry, sir, but we haven't ordered anything for Ms. Reeves. Were we supposed to?"

"No, but she received a gift basket with a card with your company name on it."

"That's odd," Penny said. "Why would someone use our name to send a gift?"

"Good question." And one he intended to find the answer to.

"Ask around the office and see if anyone else might know and call me back if they do."

She agreed, and Jacob thanked her and hung up.

"Who sent it?" Cora asked.

"I don't know." Jacob snapped a photograph of the basket. "But I'm going to have the lab analyze the food and ask Liam to dig deeper into the order to see who placed it."

CORA STRUGGLED TO understand what was happening as Jacob phoned his deputy to pick up the basket. His concern heightened her own.

Fatigue from her reaction tugged at her muscles, and she yawned into her hand.

Jacob finished the call, then joined her on the sofa again. "How are you feeling?"

"A little tired," she said. "But I'll be fine."

The look that flashed in his eyes mirrored her own fears. She almost hadn't been fine.

"Tell me what happened after you left the station," Jacob said in a quiet but serious tone.

She massaged her forehead, then relayed her movements and explained about her friend Julie.

"When did you last see her?" Jacob asked.

A fresh wave of pain splintered Cora as she recalled the way their friendship had fallen apart. "It's been over four years," she said. "This cabin was our vacation home—mine and Drew's. When Drew and I split, I moved here permanently, and Drew kept the house in Charlotte." She cringed as her accusations against Julie taunted her. "It was my fault that Julie and I haven't spoken."

Jacob stroked her arm. "Cora, none of this was your fault. Any parent who lost a child would have had a difficult time."

"But I wasn't a good friend to her," Cora said. "I thought she called Drew and told him I was crazy, because I followed this woman at the mall one day. I'm sure I seemed like a stalker."

"You're not crazy now, and you weren't then," Jacob said.

Jacob's big blunt fingers gently brushed her arm, calming her. "Fear does strange things to people."

Cora sensed he wasn't just talking about her now. "I know you suffered and miss your father," she said. "My parents died when I was in my twenties. But I lost them in a car accident. Your father was killed because someone set fire to the hospital. You must want to know who's responsible."

Emotions streaked Jacob's face. "Not knowing weighs on my mind," Jacob admitted in a low voice. "My brothers and I made a pact years ago that we'd find the person who set that fire and make him pay."

Compassion for Jacob and his brothers made her want to reach out to him. "You and your brothers are all admirable men."

Jacob gave a wry chuckle. "We're just trying to live up to my father's reputation."

"He died a hero." Cora couldn't help herself. She lifted her hand and pressed it to his cheek. "You're a good man, too, Jacob. In spite of your own tragedy, you tried to help me five years ago, and you're helping me now."

Emotions blurred as heat simmered between them. Shared pain and the need for answers had driven them both for years.

Jacob and his brothers were the most handsome, honorable men to ever come out of the North Carolina mountains.

She'd wondered why Jacob had never married. Never had a family of his own.

Now she understood. He'd devoted himself to protecting others instead of taking care of himself.

Admiration stirred, along with an attraction Cora couldn't deny. In the face of a crisis and when she'd needed him most, Drew had bailed.

But Jacob was here now. Protecting. Serving. As determined to unearth the truth as she was.

Kurt had been kind. Had vowed to help her. Had wanted more than she could give.

Because even in his kindness he hadn't heated her blood.

Not like Jacob.

He was so sexy that for the first time in years, she yearned for closeness with a man. Not just a man. Jacob.

He was kind. Caring. Loving.

His tenderness warmed her heart and made her feel as if she wasn't alone. As if she mattered. It gave her hope.

And his touch was so soothing that she craved his hands everywhere on her body.

Caught up in the feelings, she traced a finger along his strong jaw. His brown eyes darkened to black. His breath quickened. He leaned toward her.

She cupped his face in her hands and closed her lips over his.

JACOB HAD NEVER felt anything so sensual and sweet and tantalizing as Cora's tentative kiss. He should stop it, but reason gave way to passion.

He'd wanted to do this forever.

At first, in a comforting gesture. But the more he got to know Cora, the more he'd come to admire her strength and perseverance. She didn't deserve to beat herself up for not taking care of her friends when she'd been in the most horrible pain a parent could possibly fathom.

His own mother had crumbled after their father's death. She'd had health concerns before, but grief had taken its toll and her heart had given out. He'd always thought she died of heartsickness.

Cora's hand against his cheek urged him to deepen the kiss, and he traced his tongue along the seam of her mouth and probed inside. She parted her lips and accepted his sensual exploration, his chest constricting at her moan of pleasure.

He wanted more. To taste her neck and strip her clothes and touch her all over. To bring her enough pleasure to erase her fear and sadness.

She lifted her hand and threaded her fingers in his hair, and he gently pushed a strand of hair from her cheek. Her quick intake of breath suggested she liked his touch, so he lowered his head and trailed tender kisses along her throat. She tilted her head backward, allowing him deeper access, and he slid one arm behind her head to pull her closer.

Her chest rose and fell against his as their bodies touched, igniting his desire. She planted kisses on his cheek and drew him closer as he teased her earlobes and the swell of her breasts.

His body hardened. Her breathing turned raspy, and she ran her hands down his back, stroking him, firing his need.

Hunger burst inside him, and he trailed his fingers along her neck to her shoulder, then lower. But just as he started to cover her breast with one hand, a knock sounded at the door.

Jacob froze, reality interceding. Cora leaned her head against his. For a moment they stayed that way, heads touching, breathing erratic, need still simmering between them.

The knock echoed again.

"I'll get it." Jacob slowly pulled away, but tilted Cora's head to face him. "You okay?"

Her face flushed. "I'm sorry."

He bit back a comment, then strode to the door. When he opened it, his deputy stood on the other side. "You wanted me to pick up something to take to the lab?"

Jacob gestured toward the table, then retrieved the gift basket. When he glanced at the sofa, Cora had disappeared into her bedroom.

Dammit, he didn't want her to have regrets. He wanted to kiss her again. Most of all, he wanted her to *want* him to kiss her again.

But that wasn't fair and he knew it.

"What's going on with the basket?" his deputy asked.

Jacob explained about Cora's allergy and the fact that the card had been misleading. "I need to know who sent this. I'm going to get Liam to follow up on it."

"Do you think someone knew about her allergy?" Martin asked.

Good question. "It's possible. Especially considering someone tried to kill her by shooting at her."

Martin angled his body toward Jacob. "By the way, the lab called about the ballistics."

Jacob raised a brow. "And?"

"The bullet casings from Ms. Reeves's car match the one the ME removed from Kurt Philips's body."

Chapter Seventeen

Jacob's stomach clenched. "That means the same person who killed Kurt shot at Cora."

"They're still working on his computer," Martin said. "But Griff called and said the crime team recovered a key of some sort. They're trying to figure out what it goes to now."

"Did he have an office or home safe?"

"They didn't find one."

"How about his vehicle?" Jacob asked.

"A black SUV. The back window was busted out. Whoever set the fire must have looked through it."

"To get rid of evidence linking him or her to Philips's death."

"Exactly." Martin shifted.

"Find out if Philips had a safety deposit box," Jacob said. "Maybe he hid some documents or files inside."

"On it." Martin carried the basket to the door and left. As he drove away, Jacob heard the shower in Cora's bath.

He forced himself to banish images of Cora naked beneath the spray of water and ordered his libido under control.

Finding Kurt's killer might mean saving Cora's life,

so he had to focus on the investigation, not on his personal needs. Maybe there'd be time for that later.

He retrieved his laptop from his car, brought it inside and booted it up, then connected to the police database.

His conversation with Cora echoed in his head. If the gift basket was sent by the same person who'd shot at Cora, that person knew about her allergy.

Her ex-husband certainly had. And he was smart enough to create a fake account for a flower order. He texted Liam and asked him to follow up on the order from the flower shop.

Drew's wife, Hilary, would also have known about the allergy. And Cora's friend, Julie. Although Julie had her own child and hadn't adopted, so she had no motive to take Cora's baby.

The pediatric nurse was a possibility. She could have gained access to Cora's medical records and learned about her allergy through her files.

Liam was investigating Evie, so he decided to check out Faye Fuller.

She'd saved Cora's life with the EpiPen, but she could have sent the basket, then had second thoughts and changed her mind about hurting Cora.

He entered her name and ran a background search. No arrests, outstanding warrants or charges. Not even a speeding ticket.

According to Cora, Faye was frightened of her ex. He did some digging in search of the husband, but didn't find records that she'd ever been married.

He checked records for domestic violence reports and found nothing on anyone related to a Faye Fuller.

Interesting.

He continued searching, hoping to find adoption records, although the adoption could have been closed. Or…what if she hadn't obtained Nina legally?

Curious and determined to explore every avenue, he removed a handkerchief from his pocket, picked up the glass Faye had used and bagged it. He'd send it to the lab to run for prints and find out exactly who Faye Fuller was.

If she was lying to Cora, he wanted to know the reason.

As SHE SHOWERED, Cora silently chided herself for kissing Jacob. She'd never made a move on a man before, but she hadn't been able to stop herself from that kiss.

She'd slowly begun to think of Jacob as more than the sheriff. As a friend. Maybe as a lover?

You don't have time for sex or romance. Your daughter is missing. And the man who was looking for her was murdered.

Yet the two attempts on her life now made her realize she wanted to live. Not just go through the motions. For so long, she'd cut herself off from caring about anyone.

It had hurt too much to lose Alice and then Drew. She didn't think she'd survive if she lost anyone else.

Being alone had been the answer.

She dressed in clean jeans and a T-shirt, ran a brush through her hair, then studied herself in the mirror. Her cheeks were still flushed. Her eyes looked…needy.

It's okay to care, she whispered to herself. *You deserve love.*

But fear hacked at her resolve.

Jacob risked his life every day on the job. His father had died protecting others. While it was admirable, it also meant he might not come home at night. That every time he stepped out the door, he was endangering his life.

She had to keep her distance. They'd find Alice. Then she and her daughter would build a life together.

Jacob would focus on work again. Hopefully he'd even find out who set that fire and killed his father, then he and his brothers would have closure.

The sound of voices drifted to her from the living room. Was Jacob talking to someone?

Determined to refrain from throwing herself at him, she stepped through the doorway.

Jacob gripped his phone in his hand, but he wasn't talking on it. He had turned on the news. "This is a special report featuring missing persons' cases across the Southeast," the reporter said. "First we're beginning with this story which originally aired five years ago from Whistler, North Carolina."

Her heart jumped to her throat at the sight of the reporter displaying her photograph and the caption about Alice's disappearance. Cora's heart ached as she listened to the reporter recount the details of the hospital fire and Alice's abduction.

"We have established a tip line for viewers who have information regarding the cases we're featuring today and throughout this special series," the reporter said. "But first we're asking viewers to look at these projected images of what Alice Reeves Westbrook would look like over the years."

A wave of sadness mingled with hope as Cora watched. What if she had the images wrong?

The sketch faintly resembled Nina although they also resembled a couple of other little girls she'd taught.

When the latest sketch was displayed and the tip line

number flashed on the screen, she had to grip the table edge to steady her legs.

She'd been down this road five years ago. This time had to be different.

Jacob wanted to alleviate the pain in Cora's eyes, but finding Alice was the only way she'd have peace.

He phoned Liam to request information on Faye and Nina's adoption.

"On it," Liam said. "I have news on Evie Hanson. Her mother lives about thirty miles from Whistler in a retirement community. I'm forwarding you her address."

"Anything on that adoption?"

"Not yet. My forensic account is reviewing Ms. Hanson's financials. Looks like she withdrew about ten thousand dollars from her account around the time she adopted that little girl Twyla."

Ten thousand—to pay for legal fees or to buy a baby illegally?

"Did she get the child at an agency or through a private adoption?"

"Haven't determined that yet, but I'm working on it. Maybe her mother can shed some light on the situation."

"I'll drive out and talk to her now." He didn't want to waste a minute. If Evie had illegally obtained Twyla, she might be on the run.

He hung up and found Cora watching him. "Is there news?" Cora asked.

He explained about Evie's mother, Adelaide Evans. "I'm going to see her."

"I'll go with you."

His gaze was drawn to her pale pink mouth, and

memories of that kiss taunted him. He wanted to kiss her again. Promise her that he'd take care of everything.

"Maybe you should stay here and rest," Jacob suggested. "And be sure to activate the security system. Faye seems to have just walked in."

"I'm going," Cora said. "If she's reluctant to talk to you, maybe I can connect with her as a mother."

True.

She grabbed her purse and he snagged his keys, then they walked outside to his vehicle. With dusk approaching, the wind whistled off the river and cast shadows from the spiny needles of the pines across her drive and yard, which resembled long bony fingers.

Cora rubbed her arm as if to calm her nerves as he drove around the mountain. He followed his GPS onto the winding road toward the cluster of assisted living homes called Shady Oak. The mayor had spearheaded the development when his father had been diagnosed with Parkinson's. A small café, store, park and activity center added a community feel for the residents.

Silence stretched thick between him and Cora as he drove, and he forced his eyes on the road and his mind on the job so he wouldn't touch her. The SUV bounced over the ruts in the road, and he slowed to avoid a possum as he neared the turnoff to the holler.

He maneuvered the turn into the development, passed a place called The Club, where residents gathered to play games and other communal activities. Three white-haired men sat around an old whiskey barrel, engrossed in a checkers game while several women worked on a quilt on the porch.

A young woman walked beside an elderly man in

a garden by the park, and wheelchair residents were gathered by a pond.

"It looks like a nice facility," Cora commented as he parked in front of Evie's mother's cottage.

"It has a good reputation." He and Cora climbed out and walked up to the front porch. A tiny woman with a gray bun sat in a rocking chair on the front porch, her gnarled hands working knitting needles back and forth.

"Ms. Evans?" Jacob asked.

The woman dropped the needles in her lap, then tilted her head to the side. Her eyes looked glazed slightly, as if she couldn't quite focus on him. Then he realized she was blind.

"Who's there?" she called.

"It's Sheriff Maverick from Whistler, and I have a friend with me. A woman named Cora Reeves." Jacob climbed the steps slowly, so as to not startle the elderly woman.

Her rocking chair went still. "What's wrong?" she said in a harsh whisper. "Did something happen to Evie?"

Jacob stooped down in front of the woman, his instincts alert. "Ms. Evans, why would you think something happened to your daughter?"

The woman lifted a trembling hand to her mouth as if she'd said something she shouldn't have. "I… I don't know, motherly instinct, I suppose." She fidgeted with the knitting needles. "Besides, you've never come to see me before, Sheriff, so something has to be wrong." She angled her head as if staring at Jacob. "Now, where's my daughter?"

Jacob cleared his throat. "That's what I was hoping you could tell me."

Ms. Evan's lower lip quivered. "I don't know," she said in a voice that warbled. "But I'm worried."

"When did you last talk to her?" Jacob asked.

"That's just it," Ms. Evans said. "She was supposed to stop by and visit today. But she never showed up and she didn't call."

"Does she usually let you know if she's not coming?" Jacob asked.

"Yes, Evie is always dependable. She…knows I get lonely here. I live for visits from her and my granddaughter."

Jacob exchanged a look with Cora. "Do you have a number where I can reach her?"

The little woman nodded, then pulled a phone from her pocket. "She programmed it in here for me after I lost my sight."

Jacob took the phone from her while Cora sat down in the rocker beside the woman.

"I'm so worried about her," Ms. Evans said. "Two days ago, she called and was upset."

"What was she upset about?" Cora asked.

She gathered her knitting in one hand. "She was supposed to adopt a little boy, but it didn't work out."

"Did she explain what happened?"

"No, but she was devastated. And she…sounded scared, but she wouldn't say of what."

Was she frightened because the police were asking questions about her daughter's adoption?

Chapter Eighteen

Cora knelt by the woman to comfort her. "I'm sorry, Ms. Evans."

"Honey, call me Adelaide. No one calls me Ms. Evans anymore."

Cora gave her an understanding look. "I know you're worried about your daughter and granddaughter," she said, compassion for the woman filling her. "You can trust Sheriff Maverick. He's a good guy. He's been trying to help me find my missing daughter."

"What did you say your name was, dear?"

"Cora Reeves," Cora said.

Adelaide pressed a hand to her chest. "Oh my goodness. You're that woman they were talking about on the news earlier, aren't you? The one with the baby named Alice?"

Sensing the woman's agitation, Cora patted her hand. "Yes, ma'am. I've been looking for her for a long time."

Adelaide inhaled. "I remember your story from when it first aired," she said in a strained voice. "Your baby disappeared about the same time Evie was told she couldn't conceive." Her voice lowered. "That was an awful time."

"Yes, it was," Cora said, her gaze meeting Jacob's.

"I gave birth to my daughter the night of the fire, and she was stolen during the chaos."

Adelaide reached for her hand. "My daughter and I prayed for you back then," she said. "Evie was so upset that she couldn't have kids that she cried and cried for you, and then it was like a miracle. This woman she met in her support group called her and told her about this adoption. At first she was hesitant. She wanted to have a child of her own." Adelaide rubbed her chest. "But I told her that love doesn't come from genetics. It's in your heart."

Cora's throat closed. Evie had cried for her?

She'd received countless messages of support and prayers. Yet she'd also received disturbing messages where people blamed her for her daughter's disappearance. Those vile accusations had nearly destroyed her.

"Finally she opened herself up to the idea of adoption," Adelaide continued. "And she discovered it's true. She loves little Twyla like she carried her for nine months and gave birth to her herself."

Cora pictured a woman devastated because she couldn't bear children, then learning a baby was available. Evie must have jumped on the opportunity.

Had that baby been kidnapped from its mother?

JACOB QUICKLY EXAMINED the older woman's phone. There were only two numbers programmed in it—Evie's and the desk for health services at the assisted living facility.

He pressed Evie's number, but her voice mail kicked in, so he left a message. Then he called the health care office and identified himself to the receptionist.

"I'm talking with Adelaide Evans," he said. "She's

concerned about the fact that her daughter hasn't called or visited. Have you heard anything from Evie?"

"Not today. Is something wrong?" the receptionist asked.

"That's what I'm trying to figure out," Jacob said. "Ms. Evans would feel better if we could talk to her daughter. Let me know if she checks in."

She agreed and he hung up, then called Liam with Evie's number and her mother's for a trace. Technically he couldn't declare Evie missing. She was an adult and could have simply moved and not have had time to contact her mother.

But…if she was in trouble, or if she was involved in a kidnapping, she might be on the run.

Jacob stepped back to join Cora and Ms. Evans. "Your daughter didn't answer. I left a message for her to call me."

"I left her one, too," Adelaide said. "That's what worries me most. She's such a good daughter. She always calls me back."

"You mentioned she was on the verge of adopting another child. Did she use an adoption agency, or was it a private adoption?"

The elderly woman ran a finger over the Afghan she'd been knitting. "All I know is that a lawyer was handling the arrangement."

"Do you know the lawyer's name?" Jacob asked.

Adelaide rocked back and forth in the chair, obviously agitated. "She didn't say, only that she'd paid him."

Cora patted the woman's hand. Adelaide and her daughter did seem close. It was strange Evie would have moved without informing her mother of her plans.

"Tell me more about your granddaughter," Cora said softly.

"She's a sweetheart," Adelaide said. "She always brings me fresh flowers when she comes. She likes pink carnations. Lilies used to be my favorite until Twyla. Now I like carnations."

Cora smiled. "If you don't mind me asking, when is her birthday?"

Adelaide's hand fluttered her chest. "That's the funny thing. It's the same day as mine. June 8." A smile brightened the woman's face. "Evie and I thought that was a sign she was meant to be part of our family."

Cora's heart skipped a beat. Alice had been born on June 9.

Could Evie have lied about the little girl's birthday?

"There's a photograph of her on my mantel," Adelaide said. "Of course I can't see it, but Evie took it of us on our birthday, and Twyla insisted on setting it above the fireplace."

Cora exchanged a look with Jacob. "Would you mind if I looked at it?" Cora asked.

"Of course not," Adelaide said. "I love showing off my granddaughter."

A sliver of guilt streaked through Cora. Adelaide hadn't made the connection that Twyla's adoption and Cora's missing baby might be related. She didn't want to upset the woman if there was nothing to their suspicions.

"I'll get it," Jacob offered.

He slipped inside the cottage and returned a moment later with a five-by-seven silver-framed photograph. He studied it for a moment, looking back and forth between Cora and the picture.

Cora's hand trembled as she took it from him. Adelaide was grinning as her granddaughter handed her a bouquet of flowers. Cora narrowed her eyes, scrutinizing every detail of the child's face.

Her wavy blond hair was clasped in a high ponytail. She had hazel eyes and a dimple in her right cheek.

Cora's heart twisted. Could Twyla possibly be Alice?

JACOB SHIFTED AS indecision played on Cora's face. Unless her daughter looked like Cora or her ex, how could she possibly recognize her?

He left her with Evie's mother and ducked back inside the house under the guise of using the restroom. Several pictures took homage on the mantel—first, a photograph of a younger Ms. Evans and a little girl he assumed to be Evie, when Evie was about ten years old.

The second was a photograph of Evie and Twyla with a man he guessed was the husband. Jacob noted the scenery.

Mountains, a creek. A sign for Little Canoe. The couple stood in front of a cabin overlooking the theme park for children.

Did Evie own property at Little Canoe?

He searched the small desk in the living room, then the kitchen drawers for an address or reference indicating where Evie might have gone. Nothing inside but prescriptions for Evie's mother's medications, including insulin, along with bills from the facility.

He quickly searched the dresser in the woman's bedroom, but found nothing helpful. When he returned to the porch, Cora was listening to Ms. Evans relay a story.

Jacob listened politely for her to finish before he spoke. "Ms. Evans, I noticed a picture of your daughter at Little Canoe. Did she and her husband own a place there?"

She paused in her rocking. "Hmm, they bought one a long time ago, but I don't know if Evie kept it after she lost Roy. She hasn't mentioned it in a long time."

"Do you have the address?" Jacob asked.

The woman smiled. "Of course I do. I'm blind, but my memory is still pretty good." She gave him the address along with an intricate set of directions.

His phone buzzed on his hip. A text from Liam.

Got a hit on Evie Hanson. She traded her car at a used car lot for a dark green sedan. Seller said she seemed nervous and in a hurry. She was headed north.

Jacob sent him a return text. Think I know where she's going. Little Canoe. Am leaving now.

He motioned to Cora that he was ready to leave, then stooped in front of Evie's mother. "Ms. Evans," he said. "I understand that you're worried about your daughter. I'll drive up to Little Canoe and see if she's there."

The little woman pressed her hand to her chest again. "I would feel so much better if you'd do that, Sheriff."

Guilt threatened at her sincerity, but he squashed it. Work took precedence. He had to follow every lead to find Cora's baby and Kurt Philips's killer.

If Evie Hanson was involved, or in trouble, he needed to find her ASAP.

CORA COULDN'T STOP thinking about Adelaide Evans as she and Jacob drove toward Little Canoe. Adelaide seemed like such a sweet lady, a caring mother and grandmother.

If Twyla was Alice, Cora would destroy the happiness Evie had found with adoption. That bothered her more than she'd expected it to.

Still, she had to know the truth. If Twyla was her daughter and Evie had innocently adopted her without knowing she was kidnapped, she'd work with her to transition Alice. The last thing she wanted was to hurt her own child by ripping her from people she loved.

The unfairness of the situation nagged at her as Jacob maneuvered the mountain roads to Little Canoe, a resort community with year-round homes as well as rental cabins. Set at the top of the mountain, the rustic cabins offered breathtaking views of the mountain, canyon and river. Swimming, white water rafting and camping drew tourists and locals.

At Christmas, the entire community was lit up with sparkling lights and decorations. The Christmas Cottage bed-and-breakfast catered to families seeking a holiday getaway. The lighting of the fifty-foot tree in the center of Santa's village was talked about year-round.

Cora had dreamed of bringing her family here, of visiting Santa's workshop and taking a sleigh ride through the tree farm with her own children.

Jacob drove through the main village and followed the GPS onto a side street leading to a group of cabins.

"Number six," Jacob said as he pointed to a rustic ranch in the woods.

Cora spotted a green sedan parked beneath a carport. Lights from the dormer windows glowed softly against the darkening sky, making the place look homey and cozy.

Cora's pulse hammered as Jacob eased toward the

house. When he reached the end of the drive, he parked and surveyed the area.

"Looks quiet. Hopefully Evie is inside."

"Let's go see." Cora reached for the door handle and climbed out. Her legs felt shaky as they walked up to the cabin. A handmade wreath made of twigs and greenery hung on the door boasting a welcome sign.

Cora glanced toward the window as Jacob raised his fist and knocked. The blinds were closed, though, making it impossible to see inside.

The side door opened, and a woman ran toward the car, pulling a little girl behind her. They jumped in the vehicle, and the woman cranked the engine and sped down the graveled drive toward the highway.

"She's running! Let's go!" Jacob jogged down the porch steps and Cora raced on his heels. A second later, they chased the car onto the highway.

Chapter Nineteen

"Dammit," Jacob muttered as he flipped on his siren.

"That little girl is in the car with her," Cora cried. "She needs to slow down."

If Jacob hadn't been so frustrated, he would have smiled at Cora's protective tone.

"She's spooked about something." Jacob veered around a curve, tires squealing. He sped up, then blew his horn, signaling for Evie to pull over.

She maneuvered a turn, barreled over a rut in the road and nearly careened over the edge. The mountain roads were winding, forcing her to slow, but he stayed on her tail as they broke onto the main highway.

She made a sharp right to leave town, but he pulled up beside her, lights twirling, siren wailing. A mile later, he finally forced her to pull off the road into the parking lot for the Little Canoe Café. A few cars were parked in the lot, indicating some of the dinner crowd customers were lingering.

He parked beside Evie's sedan then gestured toward Cora. "Stay inside the car."

"But I want—"

"Cora, she could be armed."

"With a little girl inside?" Cora gasped.

"I don't know. Stay here for now." He gave her a pointed look. Cora wrapped her arms around her middle, her eyes sharp with fear.

Jacob climbed from his car and walked toward the sedan. Instinctively, he glanced inside. The little girl was strapped in the seat hugging a teddy bear, her head buried against the bear's head.

His heart squeezed, but he had a job to do. He rapped on the driver's window, and Evie pushed the automatic window release. Her face became visible as the window slid down. Fear streaked her eyes.

"Evie Hanson?" he asked.

She nodded. "I'm sorry I was speeding, I didn't feel well and wanted to get some medicine before the drugstore closed."

He gave her a deadpan look. "License and registration, ma'am."

"Of course." Her hand trembled as she removed her wallet from her purse and handed him her ID. It took her a minute to comb through her glove compartment for her registration, but it all matched.

"Please, if you want to just write me a ticket, I'll pay it. But my little girl—"

"Was in the car as you drove recklessly around the mountain," Jacob said sternly. "You should be more careful with her in the car."

A tear trickled down the woman's pale face. "I know and it won't happen again. Now can we go?"

"I'm afraid not," Jacob said. "Why did you run when you saw me at your house?"

"Like I said, I wasn't feeling well—"

Jacob cut her off. "Your mother is concerned about you."

Evie ran a hand over her face. "Is that what this about? Did my mother report me missing or something?"

Jacob gave a noncommittal shrug. "Actually I needed to talk to you and contacted her. She said you hadn't come by to see her and that she called and you didn't answer."

"For heaven's sake, she worries a lot now she's older. I'll phone her and reassure her that we're fine," Evie said.

"Good. But I still need to ask you some questions." Jacob gestured toward the little girl in the back. "Your daughter looks frightened, and I don't want that. Let's go inside the café, have some coffee and you can get her a treat?"

Evie nodded, although she gave him a wary look as she opened the door and slid out. He stepped aside for her to help her daughter from the car, and he motioned for Cora to join them.

The longing on Cora's face when she saw the little girl emerge from the car clutching the teddy bear tore at Jacob's heart.

Evie's eyes widened as if she recognized Cora, her fear palpable as they walked toward the café.

Cora's heart ached at the fear on Twyla's face. Being stopped by a policeman must be frightening for her.

Or was she afraid for another reason?

She wanted to comfort the child but held her distance and walked beside Jacob. Evie clutched the little girl's hand in hers, talking softly to her as they entered the café.

The heavenly scent of barbecue and apple pie filled

the air, and vases of sunflowers created centerpieces on the gingham tablecloths.

Evie ruffled her daughter's hair. "You want ice cream, honey?"

Twyla's face brightened. "Strawberry."

"You got it, kiddo," Evie said.

Jacob gestured toward a booth in the back. "There's a small arcade inside. Maybe Twyla would like to play while we talk."

Evie looked at him warily but accepted the change he offered. Then she patted Twyla's shoulder. "I'll order your ice cream while you play."

Twyla grinned, her fear dissipating as she raced to the arcade corner. Evie slid into the booth nearest the arcade, and Cora and Jacob claimed the bench seat opposite her.

A waitress appeared, and they ordered coffee and Twyla's ice cream. Jacob waited to speak until the waitress disappeared into the kitchen.

Evie fidgeted, obviously nervous. "If you want me to call my mother now, I will," Evie said. "Then can I go?"

Jacob shook his head. "A man is dead, Ms. Hanson. Cora's daughter was kidnapped five years ago. And I think you may be connected to both."

Evie gasped softly. "I don't know what you're talking about."

"Did you know a man named Kurt Philips?" Jacob said.

The waitress delivered their coffee, and Evie picked up a sugar packet, tapping it between her fingers. "No."

The slight flinch of her eyes suggested she was lying. "He was a private investigator who was searching for Cora's daughter. She was kidnapped from the hospital in Whistler the night she was born. A terrible fire broke out, injuring several people and killing some, as well."

Evie ripped the top of the sugar packet, dumped it into her coffee and stirred vigorously. "I remember the fire. That was horrible."

"You worked at the hospital around that time, didn't you?" Jacob said.

Evie twisted her mouth in thought. "Yes, but if you think I had something to do with that fire, you're wrong. I'm a nurse. I help save lives, not hurt people."

"But you were on suspension," Jacob pointed out. "So what were you doing there?"

Evie made a low sound in her throat. "I...wanted to see if I could get my job back."

"I know you're a pediatric nurse," Cora said. "And that you adopted Twyla."

Evie's eyes widened with unease. "Oh my God. You think I took your baby?"

Cora swallowed hard. "I think Kurt was killed because he discovered a lead about my little girl."

Evie leaned forward. "Listen to me, Cora, I didn't kidnap your child. I would never do that to another woman."

Cora glanced at Twyla, who was laughing at a little boy who'd joined her. Evie sounded sincere, but she kept fidgeting.

And she had run.

Was she lying to them now?

Jacob cleared his throat. "Philips contacted you, didn't he?"

Evie sipped her coffee. "He called once about a week ago and left a message."

Jacob studied her. "Did you return his call?"

She gave a small nod. "He asked about Twyla's adoption. I thought he might be working for Twyla's birth mother, that she'd changed her mind about seeing Twyla. I told him her mother signed away all her rights, that I had paperwork to prove it."

Cora bit down on her lower lip. "Her mother?"

"Where did you get Twyla?" Jacob asked.

Evie tensed. "Is that why you're here? *Does* her mother want her?"

Jacob and Cora exchanged looks. "Who is her mother?" Jacob asked firmly.

"Her name is Delaney," Evie said. "She was fifteen, pregnant and scared when I met her at the hospital. Her mother encouraged her to give her baby up for adoption."

"Did you go through an adoption agency?" Jacob asked.

"No. We used a private lawyer. But like I said, Delaney signed away all rights."

Facts could be checked. "What is the name of the lawyer?"

Evie ran a hand through her hair. "His name was Pitts. Arnold Pitts." She bit her lower lip. "Now tell me. Does her mother want her?"

"I don't know anything about this girl named Delaney," Jacob admitted. "So as far as I know, your adoption is not in jeopardy."

Unless Twyla was Alice, which he was beginning to think wasn't the case.

Still, what had Philips learned that had led him to Evie?

"Evie, if your adoption was legitimate, and you had nothing to do with the kidnapping of Cora's baby or Kurt Philips's murder, why did you run?" Jacob pressed.

"I…didn't run," Evie said although she didn't make eye contact with Jacob.

"Then why was your house completely cleaned out?" Jacob asked.

Evie looked down into her coffee again as if she could hide inside it. "I planned to adopt a little boy, but it fell through at the last minute, so I decided to get away. There's no crime in that."

"No, there isn't," Cora interjected. "What happened with the adoption?"

"Another couple got the child," Evie said, her voice cracking. "And don't ask me who, because I don't know."

"Were you working with the same lawyer you used with Twyla?" Jacob asked.

Evie gave him a wary look. "No, it was a lawyer I saw in an ad. He specialized in arranging adoptions for couples and single-parent families, so I contacted him."

"Again, why did you run?" Jacob pressed.

Evie made another low, pained sound in her throat. "Because they pressured me for more money." She stared at the window, a faraway look in her eyes. "Another couple paid twice as much as I'd agreed to, so they got the baby instead of me."

"They were selling the baby to the highest bidder?" Cora asked in an incredulous voice.

"That's what I started to think," she said quietly. "When I asked for more details about the baby's parents, the lawyer became angry. He said if I couldn't have kids of my own, I should be grateful for anyone who'd help me."

Cora sighed softly. "That was a horrible thing to say, Evie."

Evie gulped. "I told him he was unethical. That I planned to report him to the police. And...and..."

"And what?" Jacob asked.

Evie released an agonized sigh. "He said if I reported him, I'd be sorry. That... I would lose Twyla."

Jacob's heart pounded. "What he said, what he did, was very wrong, Evie. My brother is with the FBI and is investigating a baby kidnapping/adoption ring. This man may be part of it."

Evie raised a brow. "You think that baby boy was stolen?"

Jacob shrugged. "It's possible. Even if the baby wasn't kidnapped, this lawyer may be promising the child to multiple people for adoption, then pitting prospective parents against each other to inflate the price."

"I can't believe I got caught up in it," Evie said. "I lost my husband a while back, and I was desperate and...stupid."

"You're not stupid," Cora said. "That man is a vile predator."

"She's right," Jacob said. "He's taking advantage of vulnerable people, and he needs to be stopped."

"But I can't risk losing Twyla," Evie cried.

"If your adoption is legitimate, you won't lose her," Jacob assured her. "But if we don't stop him, he'll do the same thing to someone else." He paused. "Worse, if he's selling kidnapped babies, their mothers and fathers are looking for their children just like Cora is."

CORA COULDN'T IMAGINE selling babies as if they were objects. "He's right," she told Evie. "You can't allow this man to hurt anyone else."

A myriad of emotions played across Evie's face as she glanced at her daughter.

"Just think how you'd feel if someone took Twyla from you and sold her to someone else."

Evie's gaze shot to Cora's. "It would tear my heart out."

"Just like it did mine," Cora said softly. "The only thing that has kept me going is the hope of one day finding my daughter."

"Twyla isn't your child," Evie said emphatically. "I swear, I met her mother. I was there when she gave birth. I can give you her contact information."

"I believe you," Cora said, although doubts still plagued her. But she didn't want Evie to run again.

"I'll take that information," Jacob said. "I'm going to contact my brother Liam—Special Agent Liam Maverick. Then I want you and Twyla to come back to Whistler with us. Liam will find that bastard lawyer you worked with. He'll also want you to look at photographs of suspects in the kidnapping/adoption ring he's investigating." He leaned closer. "I promise, Evie, we'll keep you and Twyla safe."

Twyla raced over. "Mommy, can I have my ice cream now?"

Evie squeezed her daughter's arm. "Of course, honey. Then we're going to take a little trip."

"What is this lawyer's name?" Jacob asked.

"Tate Muldoon," Evie said in a low voice.

Jacob stood. "I'll phone Liam and give him a heads-up."

Cora waved the waitress over to bring Twyla's treat, indecision warring in her head over Evie's innocence as the waitress brought the dish of strawberry ice cream.

She chatted with the little girl about kindergarten and her favorite activities and stories as Twyla ate. Evie relaxed slightly, the love for her little girl obvious.

If Evie was in danger, she needed a friend.

But if she had some part in Alice's kidnapping or this baby ring, she deserved to go to jail.

Cora struggled to remain calm. Was this nefarious ring responsible for her baby's disappearance?

Chapter Twenty

Jacob kept an eye on Evie, Twyla and Cora as he stepped into the hall near the restroom to phone Liam. "She's scared out of her mind this guy will come after her daughter. I don't know if he'd hurt the child or just try to take her. She claims the adoption was legitimate, but we'll have to verify that."

"I'll start looking into it ASAP," Liam said. "If this lawyer is involved in the kidnapping/adoption ring, this could be a big break."

There were a lot of ifs. "Even if he's not, what he's doing sounds illegal and warrants an investigation."

"Agreed." Liam hesitated. "Do you think Evie will testify?"

"If it means protecting her daughter, yes. But we have to assure her that they'll be safe."

"I'll guard them myself," Liam said.

"Do you want me to bring them to Charlotte?"

"No, I have room at my cabin in Whistler. They can stay there."

A smart choice. It was off the beaten path, and Liam had a security system. Someone would also be pretty bold to come after Evie under an FBI agent's own roof.

Liam would make certain the mother and daughter's whereabouts remained confidential.

"All right. I'll escort them there myself."

"Copy that. What's the lawyer's name?" Liam asked.

"Tate Muldoon."

"Good work, Jacob."

"I hope it pans out," Jacob said. "And if he had something to do with Cora's baby's kidnapping—"

"He'll pay," Liam assured him.

Jacob inhaled, and they ended the call. He joined Cora, Evie and Twyla just as Twyla finished her ice cream.

Jacob grinned at the little girl. The innocence of a child's laughter and enthusiasm for simple things like ice cream warmed his heart and made him think about how lonely his house was.

He had been so focused on finding his father's killer and locating Cora's child that he hadn't made time for a personal relationship. Hadn't considered having a family of his own one day.

It had just been him and his brothers. No big holiday celebrations or family dinners. Christmas meant grabbing a beer and a burger in between jobs.

Cora looked up at him with those wide beautiful eyes, and his chest squeezed. Kissing her had been spontaneous and…nice.

Hell, who was he kidding? It was a lot more than nice. It was passionate.

He wanted to do it again.

"Everything okay?" Evie asked.

Jacob jerked his mind back to the case. "Yes. You're all set. We're meeting Liam at his place."

Wariness flashed in her eyes again, making him wonder if she was still hiding something.

Liam was an excellent interrogator. If Evie was holding back or lying, his brother would get the truth out of her.

Tension strained the air between Cora and Evie as they followed Jacob back to Whistler. Thankfully, Twyla's constant chatter and giggles eased the ride.

To soothe Cora and Twyla's nerves, Cora shared a story about a stinky skunk she'd written for her class. She'd been working on illustrations lately. Maybe one day she'd publish it.

"I loved Stinky Dinky," Twyla said. "Do you gots another story?"

Cora laughed softly. "I think I might."

For the remainder of the ride, she told stories and the three of them sang children's songs Twyla had learned in kindergarten.

But as they neared Whistler, Evie's hands tightened around the steering wheel, and her body grew rigid.

Cora patted the woman's arm. "It's okay, you can trust Jacob and his brother. They're good guys."

Evie shot her a wary look, then gave a little nod. "I hope so," she said in a raspy whisper. "Twyla means everything to me."

Tears pricked at Cora's eyes. "I understand. I really do."

Evie parked behind Jacob, her hand trembling as she opened the car door. But she lifted her chin in a show of courage as she climbed out and opened Twyla's door.

Cora followed, her emotions boomeranging in her

chest. Liam met them outside on the porch, and he and Jacob exchanged a quick brotherly handshake.

Evie squared her shoulders as if she was intimidated by Liam's size.

"You don't have to be afraid of him," Cora whispered as they walked inside. "I can vouch for the Maverick men."

Evie relaxed slightly as they entered Liam's cabin. The house was slightly larger than Jacob's, with a cathedral ceiling boasting a ten-foot stone fireplace and a deck that ran the length of the back of the house. Though it was dark, she'd heard the sound of the river outside when they parked. The back deck probably offered a view of it and the canyon below.

"You and your daughter can stay here tonight," Liam said after greeting Evie and Twyla. "There's a private wing upstairs you'll have all to yourselves."

Evie offered him a tentative smile.

"Do you have suitcases?" Liam asked.

"In the car," Evie said. "We hadn't had a chance to unpack."

"I'll get them." Jacob hurried outside to retrieve their luggage while Liam showed them around.

"The refrigerator is stocked." Liam grinned at Twyla. "I wasn't sure what you liked, but I have my favorites. Pizza and mac and cheese."

Twyla's eyes sparkled. "I love pizza and mac and cheese!"

"Really?" Liam made an exaggerated face, and Cora couldn't help but smile. The Maverick men amazed her with their bravery and kindness.

"It's been a long day," Evie said. "Is it okay if I get Twyla settled before we talk?"

"Of course." Liam gestured toward the stairs. "There are two rooms with a Jack and Jill bathroom in between. But if you're more comfortable sharing a room with her, that's fine."

Evie raised a brow at Liam as if surprised by his sensitive comment. "Thank you."

She ushered Twyla up the stairs, leaving Cora alone with the Maverick men.

Liam gestured toward the laptop on the breakfast bar. "My people have been researching Tate Muldoon."

Cora and Jacob looked over Liam's shoulder as Liam displayed a photo. "This is Muldoon meeting a woman we suspect is involved in the kidnapping ring." He hissed. "It appears the two are connected."

In the photo, the woman was holding an infant to her, the baby wrapped so tightly in a blanket that you couldn't see its face. She'd also angled her head downward to avoid direct contact with the security camera at the airport.

Cora's stomach roiled. Who did that baby belong to?

JACOB INSTINCTIVELY PLACED a hand on Cora's back to comfort her.

"Do you know how long this ring has been active?" Cora asked.

"Not yet," Liam replied. "But now we've identified Muldoon, we can dig into his background and activities."

Jacob gently squeezed Cora's arm. "He may or may not be responsible for Alice's disappearance, Cora."

Liam shifted. "But we won't rest until we have the answers."

Evie walked down the steps with a troubled expression.

"Is Twyla all right?" Cora asked.

"She fell asleep as soon as her head hit the pillow," Evie said.

"I'm sure you're tired, too," Liam said. "But I need you to look at this photograph."

Evie joined them at the computer and studied the picture of the man and woman with the baby.

"Is that the lawyer you worked with?" Liam asked.

A sick expression darkened Evie's eyes, then she murmured that it was Muldoon. "Oh my God. He's really selling children, isn't he?"

Jacob nodded. "You sensed something was wrong?"

She took a minute to answer. "Not at first, but when he started demanding more money, I became suspicious."

"How did you connect with Muldoon?" Liam asked.

Evie explained about the ad. "I realize it was stupid to choose a lawyer from an ad, but he specialized in helping bring families together. When I first spoke with him, he sounded caring, as if he enjoyed matching children who needed parents with mothers and fathers who wanted to open their hearts and homes to them."

"He's a professional. He knows how to play on people's vulnerabilities," Liam said.

"I feel like such a fool." Evie rubbed her temple.

Cora curved her arm around the woman's shoulders. "You aren't a fool. You wanted a child, and obviously have a lot of love to offer."

"You're not the only one he's done this to," Liam said. "But you can stop him from taking advantage of others by testifying against him once we make an arrest."

"I just want Twyla to be safe," Evie said. "I can't lose her."

"You're both safe here," Liam said.

"If he's running a big operation, he could have a number of people working for him," Jacob added.

"You're right." Liam checked his watch. "If my suspicions are correct, the kidnapping ring is international. They're selling babies all over the world. Transporting them across states and countries complicates the situation and makes it harder to identify and trace the children."

Jacob understood the problem. The media did what they could to broadcast nationwide, but if the babies were shipped to another country, they might never be found.

Liam glanced at Evie. "It's late. Why don't you get some rest, and I'll make some phone calls."

"Thanks." She glanced at Jacob. "And I'll call my mother." Evie said good-night and disappeared up the stairs. Liam walked Jacob and Cora to the car. Cora climbed in, but Jacob hung back to confer with Liam.

"I still think Evie is holding out on us," Jacob said.

Liam shrugged slightly. "Maybe. Let's give her some time. She's obviously frightened now and needs time to learn to trust us." He patted Jacob's shoulder. "I won't let her get away, bro. Just take care of Cora."

Liam was right. Cora was still in danger.

And he'd do anything to protect her.

CORA COULDN'T ERASE the image of Evie and Twyla's frightened faces from her mind as Jacob drove her home. Dark storm clouds rumbled above, raindrops splattering the windshield as they unleashed a torrent of rain.

Jacob snagged an umbrella from the back seat and handed it to her. She opened the door and then the umbrella before hopping out. Jacob raced to join her and they ran up the path to her porch, hunched beneath the umbrella together. She almost slipped on the wet steps, but Jacob caught her arm and steadied her.

When they reached the door, she fished out her keys while Jacob scanned the perimeter. She had set the new alarm, so she checked it as she entered. Still, Jacob motioned for her to wait at the door while he combed through the house.

"Don't you trust the system?" she asked as he returned to the foyer.

Jacob shrugged, the dim light from the porch accentuating his strong, square jaw. His eyes looked as dark and stormy as the night outside.

"I just don't want to take any chances. If Philips connected Evie to this kidnapping ring, and they know we're onto them, they may be the ones who came after you."

A shudder rippled through Cora. She dropped her purse on the end table and rubbed her arms to ward off the chill from the rain. "I can't imagine anyone so coldhearted as to steal and sell children."

A muscle ticked in Jacob's jaw. "Me, neither, although people keep surprising me. Unfortunately not always in a good way."

Despair threatened to overcome Cora as Liam's statement about transporting children to different states and countries taunted her. "If these people kidnapped my baby, she could be anywhere."

Jacob stepped closer to her, then cradled her hands between his and pressed them to his chest. "I promise you we'll find her, Cora. Keep the faith."

The conviction in his tone made her believe anything was possible.

That she might have a future filled with love and laughter again and be reunited with Alice.

She looked up into Jacob's eyes and became lost in the sensual brown depths. Jacob was one man who did what he said. Who never gave up.

A man she…was falling in love with.

Emotions glittered in his eyes as he brought her hands to his lips and kissed them. Her heart stuttered. Her breath caught.

She didn't want to be alone tonight. Jacob angled his head, his dark eyes searching hers. Asking permission?

She parted her lips on a sigh, then stood on tiptoe, cradled his face between her hands and pulled him toward her. He met her halfway.

Then their lips melded in a kiss that sent tiny bursts of desire rippling through her.

Chapter Twenty-One

Jacob had wanted to kiss Cora again ever since his lips
had first touched hers. Her sweet taste had invaded his
senses. But what had moved him the most was the fact
that she'd trusted him enough to return his kiss.

He pressed his lips to hers and drew her closer to
him, teasing her lips apart until he dove his tongue
inside. She made a low sound in her throat as if she
wanted more, and he deepened the kiss.

She threaded her fingers through his hair, and he
raked his hands down her back to her hips, pulling her
against his hardening body. Need and hunger spiked his
blood, and he walked them backward toward her sofa.

She ran her foot up his leg, tormenting him further,
and tugged at the top button of his shirt. His breath
rushed out in a burst of passion, but he forced himself
to pull back and look into her eyes.

They had to slow down, or he was going to take her
on the floor.

She clung to him with a whimper and gazed back at
him, need flashing in her beautiful eyes.

"Cora," he murmured. "We shouldn't do this."

"Why not?" she asked in a raw whisper. "We're
adults. I want you. Don't you want me?"

He arched a brow and pushed his thick length against her. "You know I do. But I want to protect you, not take advantage."

"You aren't taking advantage," she said. "I don't want to be alone tonight."

His lungs strained for air. "Are you sure?"

A smile curved her mouth, and she gave a little nod, then took his hand and led him to her bedroom. She lit a candle on her dresser, then turned to him, a vulnerable look on her face.

"It's been a long time for me," she said softly. "I haven't been with anyone since the divorce."

Her admission only fired his emotions and made him want her more. "I'm honored that you'd even consider me."

"Jacob," she said softly. "You're the most amazing man I've ever known."

His heart swelled with longing and…love. No…it was too soon to think about love.

He had to find Alice first.

But she reached for his buttons again, and he forgot about rational thought and the case and anything except holding and touching her. He removed his holster and gun and placed it on the nightstand, then stripped his shirt. The look of pure desire in her eyes nearly sent him to his knees.

No woman had ever looked at him like that.

He cupped her chin between his fingers, angled her face and kissed her again. Deep and hungry, long and sensual. His breathing turned raspy as he slipped her T-shirt over her head. His body hardened at the sight of her black lacy bra. Her breasts were full and voluptuous and overflowed the lacy barriers, her nipples stiff against the lace.

She reached for his belt and slid it off, then lowered his zipper. Just the sound of it rasping made his heart pound with excitement. He reached for hers as well, and within seconds, they'd shed their jeans and tossed them to the floor.

The scrap of black lace covering her sweet femininity elicited a groan from deep in his chest. The smile that she graced him with at the sound of his arousal made him throw her back on the bed.

Inhibitions fled as their tongues mated and danced in a sensual rhythm, and their bodies rubbed together, teasing and tantalizing, skin against bare skin.

He trailed kisses down her throat and neck to the swell of her breasts. She was the sweetest thing he'd ever tasted. He unfastened the front clasp of her bra, inhaling sharply as her breasts spilled out. Her nipples were tight and pink, begging for his mouth.

He closed his lips over the tip, suckling her and drawing one stiff peak between his lips. She moaned and raked her fingers over his back, her nails digging into his skin, urging him to continue.

He teased and tormented her until she clawed at his shoulders and wrapped her legs around his waist. He moved against her, craving her even more, and she pushed at his boxers until he shed them and tugged off her panties.

Heart racing, he climbed above her and kissed her until she begged him to join his body with hers.

CORA RAKED HER hands down Jacob's back, sensations spiraling through her. It had been so long since she'd experienced pleasure that Jacob's kisses almost sent her over the edge.

He paused long enough to roll on a condom, then rubbed his thick length against her thighs. She moaned and parted her legs, urging him to move inside her. He kissed her deeply again, his tongue mimicking their lovemaking, and she gripped his hips and pulled him closer.

He stroked her thighs again, then probed her opening with the tip of his sex, tormenting her. She closed her hand around his hard length then guided him to her.

One thrust, and she moaned his name as he pushed deeper, pulled out, then thrust inside her again. Her body quivered with excitement, passion igniting between them and urging him deeper and deeper. She wrapped her legs around his waist and clung to him as he pumped faster and harder, stirring her hunger to a fever pitch.

She murmured his name again as erotic sensations spiraled through her, and her orgasm claimed her. He buried his head against her neck as he thrust again, then he groaned her name as he came inside her.

Cora savored the feel of his warm body against hers as they clung to each other, bodies hot and intertwined, breathing ragged. Lost in pleasure, she couldn't bear to release him. She wanted him again. And again.

The thought frightened her. Yet she deserved to have pleasure, didn't she?

Jacob nuzzled her neck, then slowly extricated himself and disposed of the condom. She missed his body next to hers while he was in the bathroom, but she tugged the covers over her, still tingling from his touch.

Seconds later, Jacob crawled in bed under the covers with her and drew her into his arms. "That was wonderful," he whispered against her hair. "Are you okay, Cora?"

She curled into his arms and pressed her hand over his bare chest. She could feel his heart beating. Strong. Caring. Loving.

She felt a strong attraction that was more than physical. She liked the man. She admired him. She…wanted to be with him again.

"I forgot what it was like to be held," she said softly. "To not be alone."

His breath rasped out, and he dropped a kiss into her hair. "You don't have to be alone, not anymore."

She couldn't make promises, and she didn't expect him to. But she appreciated his words and the fact that he was still here in her bed. That he wasn't spooked by all her baggage and her emotions, and the fact that some people in town thought she was unstable.

"What about you?" she asked softly. "Why is a handsome eligible bachelor like you still alone?"

"Work."

"I don't believe that," Cora asked. "You must have women throwing themselves at you."

Jacob chuckled, then looked into her eyes. Tension and passion simmered between them, his eyes darkening with need again. "I guess I haven't met the right person," he murmured.

Their gazes locked. Cora's heart fluttered. She'd thought she'd met the right person when she married Drew. But theirs had been a whirlwind romance, and hadn't lasted. Now she realized the two of them weren't really meant for each other.

What about her and Jacob? Was it possible that Jacob might care about her more than as just a woman who needed his help?

EMOTIONS WARRED INSIDE Jacob. He was getting way too close to Cora.

Hell, they'd gotten naked and sweaty together. And it wasn't just sex, dammit. He'd made love to her.

He wanted to do it again, too. Tonight. And tomorrow.

He'd never thought about being lonely. He'd simply been alone and focused on his job. On finding the person responsible for his father's death.

But the thought of leaving Cora and not holding her again made his stomach knot.

She tilted his head down toward her and kissed him, and he forgot to think. He gave himself in to the moment, and they made love again, this time slow and languid. They took time to explore every inch of each other's bodies with slow kisses and tender touches. Her soft moans of pleasure were so titillating that he teased her with his tongue and mouth and fingers until she crawled on top of him.

He cradled her breasts in his hands, then licked each nipple, tugging one in his mouth to suckle her. She threw her head back in wild abandon, her body swaying as she impaled herself onto his erection.

He groaned and gripped her hips, thrusting into her with his whole being. His heart pounded, need and hunger driving him to increase the tempo until their bodies shook and convulsed with pleasure.

She collapsed on top of him, and he wrapped her in his arms and rolled sideways, tucking her close until she fell asleep in his arms. He hugged her next to him, knowing tomorrow he'd have to resume his role as sheriff instead of Cora's lover.

But tonight, he intended to revel in the pleasure of their bodies nestled together where they blocked out the world.

And the fact that a kidnapper might have sold Cora's baby five years ago.

Hopefully Liam and his team would crack this kidnapping ring, and Evie would divulge what she knew, and they could make an arrest. Someone, the head of the operation, or the person who'd actually stolen Cora's baby from the hospital, had to know where Alice was.

He fell asleep with dreams of bringing Cora's daughter back into her life but woke a few hours later with his mind humming that he needed to get up and get busy.

He slid from bed, then stepped into the shower. He quickly washed and dried off, then wrapped a towel around his waist just as he heard his phone ringing. He hurried to the nightstand, snatched the phone and stepped back into the bathroom to answer it.

"It's Griff," his brother said.

"Yeah?"

"IT just called about Kurt Philips's computer. They found a reference to that woman Faye Fuller."

Jacob tensed. "And?"

"She was never married. And the adoption she claims was legal was never filed. Philips suspected she might have bought the child."

Dammit. "Do you have the name of her lawyer?"

"No, that's just it. He couldn't find anything on the adoption. It was almost as if it never happened."

Maybe it hadn't. Cora had thought Faye's little girl

seemed familiar. Had been fired because she'd asked questions about her. She'd been nearly killed, and Faye was close by.

"I'll talk with her," Jacob said.

He looked up and saw Cora watching him. Her hair looked tousled, her cheeks chafed from his lovemaking. She raked her gaze over his near-naked body, and heat flared in her eyes.

He wanted to take her back to bed. Make love to her over and over.

"Jacob?"

Griff's voice jerked him back to the moment. "Yeah. Anything on that key?"

"Not yet."

"Okay, keep me posted." He ended the call, forcing his mind away from images of Cora naked and panting beneath him.

Cora inhaled. "What is it?"

He cleared his throat. "After the incident with your allergic reaction, I decided to run a background on Faye Fuller."

Cora's eyes widened. "And?"

"So far, we haven't found a record of her adoption."

Cora leaned against the doorjamb. "Then she lied to me?"

"She could have an explanation, but I'm going to question her," Jacob said.

"I'll go with you." Cora threw off her robe, turned on the shower water and climbed inside.

Jacob wanted to join her, but now wasn't the time. He had to focus.

While she showered, he dressed and made coffee. By the time she emerged in a clean T-shirt and jeans, he'd retrieved his clean clothes from his vehicle, changed into them and prepared scrambled eggs and toast.

"I'm not hungry," Cora said as she eyed the breakfast.

"Maybe not, but let's eat. It's early. Faye and her daughter may not even be up."

She reluctantly agreed and joined him at the table. A smile softened her face when he served her plate.

"And you cook? What don't you do, Jacob Maverick?"

He blushed. He wasn't accustomed to such intimacy with a woman.

"Thank you," she said as she forked up a bite of eggs.

"You're welcome." He wolfed down his food, anxious to question Faye. Cora ate hers quickly, too, then they cleared the table and headed to the door.

Silence stretched between them as they drove down the street to Faye's. Cora frowned when he pulled into the drive. "I don't see Faye's car."

"Maybe they went on an early outing," he said, although a bad feeling slithered through him.

Cora opened the door and rushed out, and he followed, the two of them hurrying to the front door. He rang the bell while Cora looked through the front window.

"I don't see anyone," she said, a shrill note to her voice.

Jacob twisted the doorknob and the door squeaked open. He motioned for Cora to stay behind him, and he eased inside. The furniture was in place, but he didn't see any toys or personal items in the kitchen or living room.

Cora's breathing rattled out and she raced to the first

bedroom. The house seemed deserted. Cora jerked open the dresser drawers and closet and turned to him with a panicked look.

"They're gone, Jacob."

Chapter Twenty-Two

Cora's heart sank. Where had Faye gone? And why had she left so quickly?

Fear for Faye and Nina struck Cora. "I wonder if her ex found her."

"Cora, there's no record that Faye was ever married."

Cora's pulse jumped. "What?"

Jacob turned her to face him. "I think she lied to you about everything. There was no abusive husband. There was no record of an adoption."

Cora's mind raced, the truth dawning on her with a wave of nausea. "No marriage or abusive husband or adoption records because…she hadn't legally obtained Nina?"

A muscle ticked in his jaw. "That's the logical conclusion."

The memory of Nina tearing her muffin like Cora did taunted her. Her drawings. The peanut allergy. Cora had sensed something familiar about the child.

But Faye had sounded so convincing about her abusive ex. Cora had started to think of her as a friend. Anger and hurt mingled with shock. "I felt sorry for her," she said. "I promised to keep her secret and be her friend. But she…lied to me and…you think she took my baby? That Nina is Alice?"

"We can't be certain," Jacob said. "Even if she did obtain her daughter illegally, it doesn't mean Nina is Alice."

Cora had been disappointed so many times that she dared not count on anything.

"What next?"

"I'm going to grab my kit from my SUV and see if I can lift some prints and collect DNA from the house. Then I'll send it to the lab, see if we can find out exactly who Faye is, and what she's running from." He pulled his phone from his pocket. "Meanwhile I'll call Liam to start a search for Faye."

"How can I help?"

"What kind of vehicle did Faye drive?"

"A gray minivan."

"Did you happen to notice the license plate?"

Cora shook her head. "I never even thought about it."

"Don't sweat it. Our tech team will find it. She can't have gone too far."

"But where is she going?" Cora said, her voice cracking.

"I don't know. Maybe she left something somewhere inside the house that will give us a hint." Jacob handed her a pair of gloves. "Put these on and look through the bathrooms and bedrooms. See if you can find a brush or toothbrush we can use for DNA analysis. Even a strand of the child's hair or Faye's can help."

Cora yanked on the gloves while Jacob phoned his brother and then hurried outside for his kit. Cora walked through the kitchen first in search of a used spoon or fork that might hold DNA, but the dishes in the dishwasher were clean. She checked the drawers, but they held cooking utensils, pot holders, dishes and a few staples.

Faye had rented the place furnished, but it also appeared that she'd wiped the counters and table down before she left.

She walked down the hall to the main bathroom and glanced at the kitchen sink. Clean, as well. She opened the medicine drawer, but barring a pack of unopened Q-tips, it was empty. The drawers in the vanity had been emptied, too. The scent of pine cleaner indicated Faye had also scrubbed the bathroom before she left.

Jacob poked his head inside the room. "Find anything?"

She shook her head. "It looks like she cleaned before she left. I'll look in Nina's room."

"Okay. I lifted a couple of prints from the doorknob and doorjamb. People usually forget to wipe those down." He hesitated. "I'll check the mother's room if you want to look through Nina's."

Cora murmured she would, then crossed the hall to the room Nina had slept in. The twin bed looked bare now, the shelves void of toys. She checked inside the dresser and closet, but they were empty.

She examined the small desk in the corner, her heart clenching when she discovered a notepad Nina had left behind. She flipped it open and smiled at the child-like drawings of herself and her mother. There were also sketches of different houses in the book, obviously places where Nina and her mother had lived.

Faye claimed she was running from her ex. If she'd gone to a shelter, she might have gotten help there. Undergroup groups helped abused women establish new identities across the country.

Or…was she really running from the law?

JACOB STOWED THE prints he'd collected in his evidence recovery kit, then shined his flashlight along the furniture in the room where Faye had slept, searching for a hair strand. The drawers had been cleaned out in the bedroom and master bath. No toothbrush, comb or brush, dammit.

Faye had left nothing behind. That fact made her behavior even more suspicious. Did she have Alice? If so, where had she gone this time?

He stooped down on the floor and shined his light along the edge of the bed. Something red caught his attention. He stretched his arm beneath the bed and his fingers touched a rain hat.

His pulse jumped, and he dragged it out and examined it. A small hair clung to the inside of the cap. He bagged the hat, hopeful it belonged to Faye or Nina, then went to find Cora.

She was sitting in the desk chair looking at something. He approached slowly, struck by her sad expression.

"What is it?" he asked.

She moved slightly to the right to offer him a view. "Nina drew these," she said softly. "There are half a dozen houses here where they lived."

Jacob squeezed Cora's shoulder. "Kids adapt."

"I know, but if Nina is my daughter, I would give her a stable home."

Jacob sucked in a breath. "I know you would, Cora. But let's find Faye. Then we'll go from there."

Cora lifted her chin in a show of bravado. She wasn't going to fall apart.

Dammit, he wanted to make everything right for her. But what if he failed?

"Did she draw or write anything in there about where she and her mother might have gone?"

"I don't see anything about the future, except Nina drew a Christmas tree in this house with a puppy beneath it. She must have hoped Santa would bring her a dog."

"Did Nina or Faye ever talk about some place they'd like to visit? Maybe a city or town or state?" Jacob asked.

Cora rubbed her temple as if her head ached. "Not that I recall."

Jacob drummed his fingers on his thigh. He hated to leave Cora alone, but if they got a lead on Faye, he wanted to pursue it without involving Cora.

"Let me drive you home. I need to take the prints and a hair fiber I found to the lab for analysis."

Cora stood and collected the sketchbook. "Whether she's Alice or not, Nina deserves to have a safe and secure home, not to be on the run."

TEN MINUTES LATER, Jacob dropped Cora at her house.

"Keep the doors locked and the security system activated," Jacob told her as he started to leave.

Nerves fluttered in Cora's stomach. She was growing accustomed to having Jacob around to protect her. But she wanted him to solve this case.

"Keep me posted."

Jacob feathered a strand of hair away from her cheek. "Of course. Hang in there, Cora."

She'd been hanging in there for five years now. But what else could she do? Falling to pieces was not an option.

As Jacob drove away, she considered calling Julie to visit, but she was too antsy to entertain anyone. She carried Nina's sketchbook to her writing desk and flipped through it again.

Her heart in her throat, she pulled out her stationery and began another letter.

> *Dear Alice,*
> *It's another beautiful summer day. I smell the flowers in the air and imagine you and me walking along the riverbank picking wildflowers to bring back and put in a vase on the kitchen table.*

She glanced out the back window and imagined building a tree house for her daughter. As a child, her father had built one for her and it had become her sanctuary. She'd climb the ladder to the inside and sit for hours drawing and daydreaming.

Most of all, she would give her little girl a home where she felt safe and loved.

Her therapist's words taunted her again. *What if you find her and she's happy and loved?*

But what if she wasn't?

She put her pen back to the paper.

> *I feel like I'm so close to finding you. I love you so much that I'll never stop looking.*

A loud knock sounded at the door. Cora startled, then

realized it might be Jacob, so she hurried to the door. But she hesitated before opening it. "Who's there?"

"It's me," a woman said in a muffled voice. "Faye."

Cora quickly unlocked the door.

Tears streaked Faye's cheeks, and she stormed in, swinging her hands in agitation. "Cora, I…didn't know where to go."

Cora closed the door, her arms crossed. "What's going on? I was just at your house and you'd packed up and moved out."

"I know, I…was scared," Faye cried. "I didn't know what to do, so I ran again."

"What are you scared of?" Cora asked. "And don't lie to me this time, Faye. I know you weren't married and there's no abusive ex."

Faye staggered back as if she'd been hit. Maybe she was wrong. Maybe Faye had changed her identity to escape her ex.

Faye rubbed her hands over her face, her face milky white.

"Talk to me, Faye. Did you lie to me?"

Faye nodded, her voice choked, "I'm sorry, I never meant to hurt you."

A sense of betrayal welled inside Cora. She wanted to scream at Faye for deceiving her. But she had to remain calm so Faye would confide in her. "Sit down and tell me everything."

Faye followed Cora to the den and sank onto the sofa, but her hands were shaking as she accepted a glass of water.

"Is there an abusive ex or isn't there?" Cora asked bluntly.

Faye shook her head, her expression pained. "Not

exactly. I made up that story because I was scared, and you were asking about Nina's adoption."

Cora sucked in a breath. "And that upset you because you didn't legally adopt her?"

Faye went stone-still, her face crumpling. "I... thought I did."

"What does that mean?"

Faye closed her eyes and sighed, then opened them and looked up at Cora. "I was distraught over my latest miscarriage," Faye said. "A couple of nights after that hospital fire, this woman approached me. She said she knew I lost a child, and that she had a baby who needed a good home. She claimed the baby's father paid her to take the child and give her away."

Cora stared at her in shock. Was she talking about Alice? "And you believed her?"

Faye nodded. "She said that the mother died in childbirth, and the father couldn't bear to look at the baby because she reminded him of his wife's death." Her voice broke. "She had adoption papers already drawn up, and I signed them and the little girl was mine."

Cora's heart pounded. Drew had been worried about his career, but he wouldn't have paid someone to take Alice away.

Would he?

Perspiration beaded Cora's neck. "Where is Nina now, Faye?"

Faye released a sob. "That's just it. I don't know where she is."

Panic shot through Cora. "What do you mean?"

Faye's voice cracked. "Last night, I got this threatening phone call warning me that if I talked about the adoption, I'd be sorry. So early this morning, I packed up Nina and told her we were taking a trip."

Cora's blood went cold. "Go on."

Faye swiped at tears. "On the way out of town, someone ran me off the road. I hit a ditch and blacked out. When I came to, Nina was gone."

Chapter Twenty-Three

Jacob met Liam at the sheriff's office to hand over the evidence he'd collected at Faye's house.

"How are Evie and her little girl?" Jacob asked.

Liam shrugged. "Fine. I left her with your deputy looking over mug shots of suspected child kidnappers."

Jacob explained about finding Faye's place empty. "See if Evie recognizes Faye or if there's a connection between the two of them. Faye had miscarriages and Evie couldn't have children. Maybe they met at a support group or a fertility clinic or something." That was a long shot, but Jacob couldn't ignore any possibility, no matter how remote.

"I'll ask her," Liam agreed.

Liam's phone buzzed, and he checked the text, then returned one. A second later, Liam addressed Jacob. "The analyst found a file about Drew Westbrook and his wife. Philips was supposed to meet with him for questioning the morning of the day he died."

Jacob had disliked Cora's ex from the beginning. How could you respect a man who abandoned his wife when she was grieving for their kidnapped child?

Some men wanted a namesake. Perhaps he'd been disappointed Cora had delivered a daughter?

Acid boiled in Jacob's blood as Liam described the man's findings. If Drew Westbrook orchestrated the kidnapping of his own child, he was a cold-blooded monster. He'd nearly crushed Cora.

Jacob would see the damn man behind bars.

"I'm going to question him, and this time he'd better talk," Jacob said.

Jacob rushed outside to his car, then dialed Cora. But she didn't answer.

Dammit. If something had happened to her, he'd never forgive himself.

A minute later, she texted him. Call you in a minute.

Relief spilled through him. At least Cora was safe.

CORA BARELY CONTROLLED her panic. "Who was the woman who gave Nina to you?"

"She said her name was Valerie and that she worked for an attorney who'd already drawn up the adoption papers."

"And you believed her?" Cora asked.

Faye's face wilted. "I know it was stupid, but at the time I was so desperate for a child I didn't question her. She seemed truly afraid that the father would hurt the child if I didn't take her. So I didn't lie about being afraid the father would come after Nina."

"Why did she offer you the baby? Did you know her?"

Faye massaged her temple. "After the last miscarriage, I met her in the waiting room at my counselor's office."

"So she knew you'd lost a child?"

Faye twisted her hands together. "Yes, I told her everything. She seemed so…nice."

Suspicions reared their ugly head in Cora's mind. Valerie had papers from an attorney. Drew was a lawyer. No…she couldn't believe he'd give their child away…

She gritted her teeth. "What was the attorney's name?"

Faye rubbed a hand over her eyes. "I really don't remember. That night is a blur."

"Think, Faye, this is important. He and this woman may have been working together."

"I'm sorry," Faye said, her voice breaking. "I believed her, but I realize now I was wrong. I had no idea she stole Nina."

A chill rippled through Cora. "Is Nina my daughter?"

Tears trickled down Faye's cheeks. "I'm not sure, but I think so."

Cora's breath caught. She had finally found Alice?

Faye cleared her throat. "When you started asking questions and I saw the drawings you did of Alice, and then your allergy… I started putting it together." She released a sigh. "Then the phone calls started."

"What phone calls?"

"From the woman. She warned me to keep my mouth shut or I'd be sorry."

Cora swallowed hard.

Faye's chin quivered. "Cora, I think she tried to kill you and she sent you that basket, and that she killed that private investigator because he found out about her."

Terror clawed at Cora. "Oh my God," Cora whispered. "And this woman has Nina now?"

Faye released a sob. "I'm afraid so."

Cora barely suppressed a scream. "Do you know how to contact this woman?"

"No," Faye said brokenly. "She called from an unlisted number."

Fear seized Cora. "Where do you think she'd take Nina?"

"I have no idea," Faye cried.

"We have to call Jacob. His brother is with the FBI. They can issue an Amber Alert and start looking—"

"No, she might hurt Nina."

Anger rooted itself deep inside Cora. "And if we don't, she may take her someplace where we'll never find her."

Faye looked miserable, but she finally agreed. Cora punched Jacob's number, pacing as she waited for him to answer. He picked up on the third ring.

"Cora?"

"Jacob… I think Nina Fuller is Alice. Faye is here," she said in a choked voice.

"Whoa, slow down. Did Faye tell you Nina is your daughter?"

Cora relayed Faye's story. "Faye thinks this woman killed Kurt and she tried to kill me, and now she has Nina. You have to find her, Jacob. She sounds crazy."

"Tell me everything you know," Jacob said.

"The woman claims her name was Valerie. Faye can't remember the lawyer's name."

"Does she still have the adoption papers?" Jacob asked. "They would have the lawyer's name on them."

Cora covered the phone with his hand and asked Faye about the papers.

Her face paled. "I…put them in a safety deposit box."

Hope sprouted in Cora's chest. "Then we'll go get them."

"Cora?"

She passed on the information. "Faye and I will get the papers and call you back with a name."

"All right. Meanwhile I'll get an Amber Alert issued."

"Jacob, Faye said the woman told her the baby's mother was dead, and that the father paid her to take the child. What if that lawyer—"

"Was Drew?" Jacob finished. "I'm almost to his place now. Don't worry, if he's involved, he'll talk."

Cora hung up, emotions threatening to overcome her. She couldn't bear to think that the man she'd once loved and married would sell their child.

If he had, she wanted him to pay.

She looked up at Faye and saw the misery on her face. Misery because she loved Nina.

She'd betrayed Cora by lying about being afraid of an abusive ex.

But she was here now. Telling the truth. Asking for her help to find her daughter.

Their daughter.

She had to put her own feelings aside. Once Alice was safe, she and Faye would talk about the future.

But first they had to find Alice…

ANGER RAILED INSIDE Jacob as he drove toward the Westbrook house. He phoned Liam and explained the situation. Liam agreed to issue the Amber Alert and to post Nina's picture on the news.

"That son of a bitch," Jacob said. "If he's behind this, he's going to find out what it feels like to be behind bars."

With every passing mile, Jacob's anxiety rose. He

tried not to imagine the worst-case scenarios, but they taunted him, intensifying his fear.

Cora may have overreacted in the past, but this time she'd been right. The girl down the street had been her missing daughter. She'd felt a connection.

He had to bring her home safely to Cora.

But what about Faye? If she truly hadn't known Nina was kidnapped, she was a victim in the situation, too. And what about Nina? She loved Faye and thought of her as her mother...

He maneuvered the last turn down the drive to the Westbrooks, steeling himself against punching the bastard. He had to remain professional. Persuade him to talk.

Confess.

Drew's Mercedes sat in the front circular drive.

His phone buzzed with another text. Liam with news about Philips's computer. He skimmed the information, his pulse hammering.

Jacob parked behind the Mercedes, adjusted his weapon, clipped his phone to his belt, then climbed out and walked up to the front door. He rang the doorbell, shifting to survey the land. He didn't see Hilary's car, but the garage door was closed, so her vehicle could be tucked inside.

The door opened and Drew stood on the other side, his brows knitted in a frown. He wore dress slacks and a collared shirt suggesting he'd been at the office or was heading there.

"Mr. Westbrook," Jacob said. "We need to talk."

Drew tunneled his fingers through his neatly clipped hair. "What now?"

"Let me come in and I'll explain."

"If you came to accuse me of killing Kurt Philips again, I'll phone my lawyer."

Jacob swore silently, then elbowed his way past the man. Westbrook closed the door and spun toward him. "Listen to me, Sheriff Maverick, I'm fed up with—"

"Shut up," Jacob said, barely holding onto his temper. "Your daughter may be in danger."

Drew's face went stark white. "What the hell are you talking about?"

"We found notations in Philips's files indicating that he'd uncovered evidence implicating you in your daughter's kidnapping."

"That's impossible," Drew shouted. "Because I wasn't involved!"

The man sounded convincing, but he could be adept at lying. "Really? Because we think we know who adopted her, and she claims the baby's father didn't want her."

"What?" His voice rose. "That's insane. I loved my baby. Now, who has her?"

"I don't believe you." Jacob jabbed Drew in the chest. "I think you wanted your career more than you wanted a family and you gave this woman money to get rid of Alice so you could make partner."

Chapter Twenty-Four

Worry nagged at Cora. How could they find Nina when they had no idea who this woman Valerie was? If she was desperate, which she must be to have kidnapped Nina, she could be anywhere.

For God's sake, she could be hopping on a plane to a foreign country.

Panic made her heart pound as she drove Faye to the bank to access her safety deposit box.

She remained in the lobby while Faye met with the bank manager, then Cora followed her to retrieve the papers.

Frustration knotted Cora's insides as Faye read the name on the documents. Tate Muldoon.

She searched her memory banks in case he worked with Drew, but she didn't recall a lawyer named Muldoon. Although hadn't Evie mentioned Muldoon?

"I'm texting Jacob the lawyer's name. If he can find him, maybe he can force him to talk."

Faye nodded and closed the safety deposit box while Cora sent the text.

She and Faye walked outside to the car together, but she was at a loss as to what to do now. They could go back to her house and wait.

She'd been waiting for so long…

"Why don't you try to sketch what this woman Valerie looks like," Cora suggested.

"I'll try but it was a long time ago."

Faye's phone buzzed just as they settled in the car. She snatched it from her purse, her face paling as she read the message. She angled her phone toward Cora.

If you want to see Nina again, do exactly as I say. Meet me and bring Cora Reeves with you. No police or you'll never see the little girl again.

JACOB SCRUTINIZED DREW'S reaction for a tell that the man was lying. But he seemed genuinely upset.

Because he was innocent or because he'd been caught?

"Look, Drew," Jacob said, forcing a calm tone, "if you tell me everything now, tell me where this woman has taken Nina Fuller—Alice—I'll see about cutting you a deal."

"I don't need a damn deal," Drew bellowed. "Because I had nothing to do with my baby's kidnapping. And if I knew where she was now, I'd be in my car on the way to get her." He paced, sweat trickling down the side of his face. "I know you think I was cold and that I should have stayed with Cora, but it was just too damn hard. I loved my baby, and I felt guilty for not protecting her. And not because I paid someone to take her. Because I was her father, and fathers are supposed to protect their children." He sank onto the sofa and dropped his head into his hands. "I would have done anything to have found Alice. It just hurt too much to look at Cora every day, because it reminded me that I'd failed her, too."

Jacob breathed out. "You certainly moved on quickly."

Drew pinched the bridge of his nose. "It may seem that way, but I never stopped loving Cora. We were both such a mess, though, and when I tried to help her by cleaning out the baby room, she accused me of not caring, of forgetting about our baby." He pounded his chest. "But I never forgot. Not for a moment."

"You have another child," Jacob said.

"Yes, and I love him. But he didn't replace my daughter." He scrubbed at his face and the tears tracking his cheeks. "Now please tell me. Do you know who took Alice and where she is?"

Jacob read the lawyer's name that Cora messaged him. "I was hoping you could help with that."

"But I don't know anything," Drew said between clenched teeth.

Jacob released a breath. He didn't like Drew, but he was starting to believe him. "She told the woman who thinks she adopted your daughter that her name was Valerie."

Drew's brows knitted in a frown. "I don't know anyone named Valerie."

"What about a lawyer named Tate Muldoon?"

Drew frowned. "No. I've never worked with anyone by that name."

Jacob glanced around the room. "Is your wife here?"

Drew shook his head. "She dropped our son at the nanny's because she had a luncheon with her friends. Why are you asking about Hilary?"

"She was at the hospital the night Alice was kidnapped. She also worked with you before the kidnapping."

"So? A lot of people worked with me. She was there to congratulate me and Cora."

Jacob shook his head. "We looked back at security cameras and found a woman dressed in scrubs carrying a bundle through the downstairs laundry area. We think that woman may have kidnapped Alice."

For the first time since he'd met Drew, hope brightened the man's eyes. "Did you identify her?"

Silence stretched between them for a long minute. "No, but I have an idea who she is."

Drew stood up and fisted his hands by his sides. "Dammit, Sheriff, stop beating around the bush and tell me everything you know."

Jacob stared into the man's eyes, gauging his reaction. "I think the woman in the scrubs was your wife."

Drew staggered backward as if he'd been punched. "Hilary?"

"Yes," Jacob said.

"That's crazy," Drew said. "Hilary would never do something like that."

"She was at the hospital the night Alice was born, then disappeared when the fire alarm sounded. And according to the private investigator's notes, someone at your office suggested Hilary was interested in you before your baby was taken." The pieces clicked together in Jacob's mind. Now he had to make Drew see the truth. "He also uncovered a police report regarding Hilary when she was in college. Apparently she was obsessive about a guy she met, and began stalking him. He had to take out a restraining order because she became violent."

"My God," Drew said, his voice edged in disbelief. "I had no idea."

Jacob gave him a moment to absorb the revelation. "What if Hilary took your baby and gave her away in order to break up your marriage?"

Drew shook his head in denial, although Jacob saw the wheels of suspicion begin to turn in the man's mind. "But she tried to console Cora…and me."

Jacob raised a brow. "You were both distraught. Her scheme was working. So she comforted you. That was part of the plan, too. You were vulnerable, and she stepped in to hold your hand. It was her way of winning your affection."

Emotions darkened Drew's eyes. "No…she wouldn't…"

"Has your wife been acting strangely lately? Nervous?"

Drew's gaze locked with his, the fear in his eyes palpable, as if he realized the woman he married might be a cold, calculating monster. "Well…after you left the other day, she accused me of still being in love with Cora."

Jacob's gut knotted. Was he?

"Someone tried to kill Cora, Drew. Twice. I believe it was because Kurt Philips was on the verge of revealing who took your baby. If Hilary thinks you still love Cora, that could have been a double blow. She may have feared she was about to get caught and that she was going to lose you. So she panicked."

"My God, I…just can't believe Hilary would do that. She had my son—"

"Not long after you were married," Jacob said. "Another clever ploy. Giving you what you lost cinched the deal for her. Having a child with her meant that you'd never reconcile with Cora."

Drew leaned over, breathing deeply as if he was going to be sick.

"We need to find your wife," Jacob said. "Where is she?"

"I told you, having lunch with her friends," Drew said, his voice strained.

"Then call her." Jacob shifted. "Do it now, Drew."

Drew nodded and reached for his phone.

He pressed his wife's number and put it on speakerphone. But the phone rang and rang, and no one answered.

CORA BATTLED COMPLETE panic at the idea that this woman would hurt a child. What kind of horrible person was she?

Someone who'd tried to kill her because Kurt had figured out her identity.

"I have to call Jacob," Cora said. "We could be walking into a trap, Faye. This woman might kill us both. Then what would happen to Nina?"

Faye clasped her hand, terror emanating from her. "You heard what she said. Do you want to get Nina hurt?"

Cora barely resisted correcting her and telling her Nina's real name was Alice. "No, of course not," Cora snapped. "More than anything I want my baby back."

Faye's gaze latched with hers. A mixture of fear, pain, regret, even sympathy rippled between them.

Cora's throat closed. They were two mothers who loved one little girl. Saving Nina—Alice—was all that mattered.

"Please," Faye cried. "I couldn't stand it if anything happened to my—our—daughter."

Tears pricked Cora's eyes. "All right. Let's just go to the location she texted you. Do you know where it is?"

Faye shook her head. Cora entered the address from Faye's phone into her GPS, then started the engine and pulled away from the bank. They headed north, deeper into the mountains.

Cora's phone rang as she veered onto the mountain road. Jacob.

The temptation to answer it seized her full force. She wanted to hear Jacob's voice. Have his expertise on her side. Know he was behind her and with her, and that he would be there to rescue Nina. Alice.

God, they had to find her. Save her.

Faye twisted a tissue in her hands. "I can't imagine what you've been through," Faye said. "I swear to you, Cora, I didn't know Nina was kidnapped."

Tears blurred Cora's vision at the sincerity and anguish in Faye's voice. Cora wanted to be angry with her for having the last five years with Alice, years she'd missed.

But if Faye hadn't adopted Alice, someone else might have. Someone who might not have loved and cared for her and protected her as Faye had. Nina was strong and confident and funny and creative—an amazing kid. She had Faye to thank for that.

Thunderclouds darkened the sky, threatening rain, and they fell into silence as she concentrated on driving. The winding mountain roads were treacherous and dangerous enough without a storm.

She clenched the steering wheel with a white-knuckled grip. She had to get them safely up the mountain.

Although fear consumed her. She and Faye might be walking into an ambush. This woman had killed Kurt and tried to kill her twice.

Who would raise Alice if something happened to her and Faye?

JACOB PHONED CORA to see if she'd heard something from Nina's kidnapper, but she didn't pick up. Dammit, where was she?

He left her a message warning her that he suspected Hilary was behind the kidnapping, then asked her to call him.

"Cora didn't answer," Jacob told Drew. "Any word from your wife?"

"No," Drew looked defeated. "I've called all her friends. She didn't make their luncheon today, and no one has heard from her."

"Drew," Jacob said, struggling to remain calm. "Is there a place where Hilary would go if she wanted to be alone? Do you two own another home or vacation property?"

Drew leaned his head into his hands, shaking his head back and forth as if tormented. When he raised his head and looked at Jacob, tears filled his eyes.

"I can't believe she'd do this. But if she has Alice, I want you to find her."

"A place? An address?" Jacob asked.

Drew rose and walked over to the corner. He opened a desk drawer, rifled through some papers, then turned back to Jacob.

"Hilary's family owned a place in the mountains. She inherited it when they died last year."

"Where is it, exactly?"

Drew swiped a hand over his eyes. "It's up north. It's a little hard to find, but I can take you there. We visited once with her family when we were first married."

Jacob snagged his keys from his pocket. "Let's go. If she has Alice and she's scared we're on to her, Alice might be in danger."

Jacob raced outside to his police car, anxious to get on the road. Every minute that passed meant Hilary was getting farther and farther away with Cora's daughter.

Chapter Twenty-Five

Nerves tightened every muscle in Cora's body as she drove up the mountain. Dark clouds threatened to unleash rain on the winding road and lightning zigzagged across the foggy sky.

She prayed it held off. Rain would make the roads more treacherous. She sped around a curve, struggling to keep the car on the highway around the switchbacks.

The GPS directed her to turn onto a side road that seemed to disappear into the thick woods. Trees shrouded the light, the branches clawing at her as if they were long arms and hands trying to keep her from reaching her daughter.

Faye sat stone-still, her fear palpable.

Finally they reached another turn that wound up a long hill and ended deep in the forest. A rustic cabin was perched on the side of the mountain, and a gray SUV was parked sideways near the front door, as if the driver had been racing to get inside the house.

Cora's heart pounded as she rolled to a stop and threw the gearshift into Park.

"She can't have hurt Nina," Faye said in a raw whisper. "She just can't."

Cora gripped Faye's hand for a minute. She wished

Jacob was here, but the woman had said no police and she couldn't take any chances with her daughter's life.

Cora gathered her courage. "Let's go."

Faye climbed from the passenger side, and they walked up to the door together. The shades were drawn, the dark sky adding an eerie feel that sent a chill through Cora.

She knocked on the door, then Faye reached out and pushed it open.

Before they could step inside, the shiny glint of metal flashed, then Drew's wife ordered them to come in.

Dear God. Hilary. She was behind this.

Faye exchanged a terrified look with her, fear clawing at Cora. But she'd do anything to save her little girl.

The composed, well-manicured and polished Hilary had disappeared. In her place stood a crazed, disheveled-looking woman waving a gun in their faces.

"Where's Nina?" Faye asked.

"She's safe in the other room," Hilary said shrilly. "She'll stay that way as long as you do as I say."

"She must be frightened," Cora said. "You have a child of your own, Hilary, don't hurt her."

"I told you that she'll be fine if you cooperate."

"What do you want us to do?" Faye asked in a shaky voice.

Hilary motioned for them to move into the den where she'd drawn all the curtains.

"Tell me," Faye cried.

Hilary spun toward her, the gun raised. "I'll let you go if you take Nina and leave town. Go far, far away and keep your mouth shut."

Faye's eyes darted toward Cora. "But what about Cora?" Faye asked.

A bitter laugh escaped Hilary, cutting into the strained silence in the dreary interior of the cabin.

Hilary barked a sarcastic sound. "She's going away for good."

Cora steeled herself against reacting. If she was going to die, she wanted answers. "You killed Kurt, didn't you? Then you tried to kill me."

"You wouldn't stop looking for that baby," Hilary cried. "I thought you'd give up eventually, and Drew would see how crazy you were, but no, you were so damn persistent."

The truth dawned on Cora. "You told Drew about that day at the mall, not Julie."

"He had a right to know how unstable you were."

"Because you kidnapped my child," Cora said, rage hardening her tone. "Did you and Drew plan it together?"

Another bitter laugh, almost maniacal. "Ha. Drew had no idea. I fell in love with him the minute we met. I knew I could help him reach his career goals, and that you didn't care. All you talked about was having a kid."

Cora clenched her hands by her sides. Drew hadn't known?

Hilary waved the gun in Cora's face, her eyes wide with rage and hatred. "I knew when you had that baby, he'd never leave you, that you were going to ruin him. He'd never have made partner so quickly if he'd stayed with you and been saddled with a kid."

"But you had a child with him a year after you married," Cora said, anger surfacing through the shock.

Hilary paced in front of the fireplace, her arm jerking as she waved the gun back and forth between Cora and Faye. "Only because he felt so damn guilty over you and that baby of yours. I figured the only way to help him get over it was to give him another child."

Tears burned Cora's eyes. "Does he know what you did?"

Hilary paused in front of Cora, the gun aimed at Cora's head. "No, and he never will!"

"Don't do this," Faye pleaded. "It's not right, Hilary. Think about your little boy."

"I am," Hilary shouted. "He needs for me and his father to stay a family." She turned a hate-filled look at Cora. "That means I have to get rid of you."

JACOB SPED TOWARD the cabin Hilary's parents owned, hoping Drew wasn't leading him astray. If Drew was lying about not knowing what Hilary had done, he could be guiding him into the wilderness to kill him and dispose of his body where no one would ever find him.

But Drew's anguish and shock seemed too real to be faked. The man literally looked physically ill.

Jacob's phone buzzed as he climbed the mountain. Liam. He pressed Connect. "I'm driving. You're on speaker."

"I got your message about Hilary Westbrook. We're closing in on Muldoon. If he faked adoption papers for Alice, he's been at this a lot longer than we thought."

"Good. We're on our way to find Hilary," Jacob said.

Drew made a pained sound in his throat.

"Drew's with me. Hilary's family owns a cabin in the northern part of the mountains. We're on our way there now."

A tense heartbeat passed. "Send me the coordinates and I'll meet you there. This woman sounds dangerous."

Jacob glanced at Drew, who gave a nod as if consenting for Liam to provide backup.

"I don't know the exact address," Jacob told him.

Drew cleared his throat. "The house is owned by Selma and Wilton Jones," Drew said. "It's off Route 5."

"Thanks. I'm on my way."

The line went dead, and Jacob glanced at Drew, his stomach twisting. "She won't hurt Cora or the little girl, will she?"

Drew looked at him blankly. "I have no idea. If she stole Alice, apparently I don't know my wife at all."

"PLEASE, HILARY," CORA PLEADED. "Think of Drew. When he learns what you did, he'll want to know where his daughter is. If you hurt her or Faye, or me, he won't be able to forgive you."

"He won't find out," Hilary screamed. "He won't, because you'll be dead and Faye and her daughter will be gone." She glared at Faye. "And if Faye tells anyone, I'll kill her, too."

"Put the gun down," Faye said. "You don't have to kill anyone, Hilary. Cora can go away just like me, move to another state, and your secret will be safe."

"You're lying," Hilary bellowed. "You and Cora will go to the police!"

She swung the gun toward Cora and aimed. Faye suddenly lunged at Hilary. Cora screamed, "No!"

Faye tried to knock the gun from Hilary's hand, and they struggled. She pushed Hilary against the wall, but the gun went off. Faye cried out and collapsed, one hand clawing at Hilary. Hilary shoved her away, and Faye dropped to the floor, her hand covering her chest where blood gushed.

Hilary staggered from the wall, her face etched in shock, her hand jerking as she still clenched the gun.

Cora ran to Faye, dropped down, then grabbed a pillow from the sofa and pressed it over Faye's chest. She placed Faye's hand on top of the pillow. "Keep pressure on it, Faye. I'll call for help."

"Save Nina," Faye reached for her hand. "Save our daughter, Cora. Please. Save her and love her for me."

Tears burned Cora's eyes. She wanted to help Faye, but she had to rescue Nina from this madwoman. Then she could phone an ambulance.

Hilary was staring at her gun hand and the blood, as if she was dazed and confused. Cora had to hurry.

She jumped up and ran down the hall. "Nina?" she called as she entered the first bedroom.

No answer. Please, dear God, Hilary hadn't hurt her, had she?

Trembling with fear, she tried the closet, but it was empty. Adrenaline pumped through her, and she ran to the last bedroom. "Nina, if you're in here, call out!"

Silence.

Fear drove her to cross the room, and she checked that closet. Nothing. Terror pounded in her heart.

She ran back to the hall and noticed a door, then opened it. An attic. She raced up the steps, the darkness engulfing her and adding to her terror. "Nina?"

A low sound. A cry.

Cora almost burst into a sob. She had to get Nina out of here. She raced across the room and opened the door to another closet. It was so dark inside she could hardly see.

"Nina?"

A whimper.

"Nina, it's Cora Reeves are you in there, honey?"

"Ms. Reeves?"

It was the faintest whisper of her name, but relief surged through Cora. She knelt and reached out her hand. "Come on, sweetie, we have to hurry!"

Nina took her hand. The little girl's fingers were icy, and her legs almost gave way. Tears tracked her cheeks, but Cora gave her a quick hug.

"Where's Mommy?" she cried.

I'm right here, Cora said silently. But Nina was talking about Faye. "We're going to get out of here, then find her."

She clasped Nina's hand, ran down the steps, then veered down the hall toward the rear. But just as she and Nina reached the back door, Hilary pressed a gun to Cora's temple.

"Walk into the woods," Hilary ordered.

"Ms. Reeves," Nina cried.

Cora squeezed Nina's hand and pulled her against her. "Stay close to me, sweetie."

"Walk," Hilary ordered.

Cora scanned the dark woods, debating what to do. If they made it deeper into the trees, she could trip Hilary up, then she and Nina could run back to the car.

She'd just found her daughter. She couldn't lose her.

She wrapped one arm around Nina's small shoulders. Nina's body was shaking, her lower lip quivering. She wanted her mommy, Faye. But Cora had no idea if Faye was still alive.

One step. Two. She trudged deeper into the thicket of trees. Leaves crunched and twigs snapped beneath their feet. A breeze picked up, stirring the brush, and thunder boomed in the sky.

The sound of the water rippling over rocks echoed in the wind. Another few steps, and Hilary halted. Cora's breath lodged in her throat. They'd reached the edge of a cliff.

She inhaled, desperate to save Nina. Alice. They were one and the same. All the letters she'd written to her daughter and the presents waited.

She turned, determined to make one more plea. "You can do anything you want with me, Hilary, but promise me you won't hurt Nina."

"You just couldn't give up, could you?" Hilary said in a rage-filled whisper. "If your little girl dies, it's your fault."

Then Hilary raised the gun and fired.

Chapter Twenty-Six

Jacob eased up the drive to Hilary's cabin, scanning the area for an ambush. Hilary was a desperate woman. It was possible she'd hired someone to help her escape justice.

Her husband was a criminal defense attorney. He knew people who would work for hire. She'd worked at his law firm and knew how to access information. She could have snuck into Drew's files or on his computer at any time.

Cora's car was parked behind a gray SUV.

"That's Hilary's car. She drives it instead of the minivan when she meets her friends," Drew said in a strained tone. "Do you want me to call her?"

Jacob debated on the effectiveness of a call as compared with a surprise attack.

"I think seeing you in person might be our best bet. If she did all this for you, maybe you can get through to her." Jacob narrowed his eyes. "But it could be dangerous."

"I don't care." Anger sharpened his voice "I'll do anything to save Alice."

Jacob gave a clipped nod. "Her name is Nina now,"

he said quietly. "That's what the woman who adopted her calls her. Nina."

Pain streaked Drew's face. "Cora knows this now?"

"She suspected. We figured it out. I'm sure she came here to rescue your daughter."

"God, she's the strong one," he said brokenly.

A gunshot blasted the air as Jacob climbed from his SUV, and pure terror seized him. Drew cursed and jumped from the vehicle.

"It came from the woods." Jacob removed his service revolver from his holster and clutched it at the ready. Drew started ahead but Jacob grabbed his arm. "She's armed, Westbrook. Stay behind me."

Drew growled another obscenity, and the two of them scrambled around the side of the house. The wind whistled, and lightning zigzagged above the trees.

The sound of a scream reverberated over the rustle of the branches. "That way." Jacob hooked his finger toward the right and pushed Drew behind him again. He eased forward, ducking from tree to tree until he spotted Hilary, who was waving the gun like a crazy woman.

"You can't hide forever!" she yelled. "I'll find you and it'll all be over."

Drew lurched forward. "Hilary, stop it!" Drew shouted. "Drop the gun!"

Jacob searched the darkness for Cora and Nina but didn't see them.

Hilary whirled toward her husband, eyes crazed. "What are you doing here? You weren't supposed to come!"

Drew held up a warning hand, inching closer. "You kidnapped my baby five years ago, Hilary. How could you do that to me?"

"I loved you," Hilary cried. "I always did. I was the one who was supposed to help you climb to the top, but you married that woman instead."

Drew inched another step closer, his voice low. "So you stole my child to break up my marriage?"

"I had to show you that you were supposed to be with me," Hilary said, her hand bobbing with the gun. "And then you did see…"

"You wrecked my life, and you devastated Cora. That was cruel, Hilary." He fisted his hands by his sides.

Jacob braced his gun to shoot the woman, his gaze still scanning the woods.

Dear God, Cora had to be all right. He was in love with her. He had been for a long time. And he'd never told her how he felt.

They knew who her daughter was now. She had a chance to know her, to love her little girl, to make up for lost time.

"For God's sake, Hilary," Drew said. "Cora and I were crazy with worry and fear. We didn't know if Alice was alive or dead. And you knew all along and stood by and watched us suffer."

"I consoled you, then I helped you make partner. Don't you see? Taking your baby was the best thing for you. It garnered you all kinds of publicity and sympathy."

Rage filled Drew's eyes. "I didn't want to make partner by having people pity me." He stepped closer. "You know I had nightmares about what might have happened to Alice. Terrible, horrible nightmares that she might be hurt or thrown away in a ditch somewhere."

"I gave you a baby!" Hilary screamed, venom in her voice.

A movement to the left caught Jacob's eyes, and he eased toward it. Relief surged through him when he spotted Cora stooped down, hiding behind a boulder. The little girl was tucked beneath Cora's protective embrace. But where was Faye?

Jacob aimed his gun at Hilary, squared his shoulders and crept into the clearing. "It's over, Hilary. Put the gun down and let's end this peacefully. No one has to get hurt."

"No, I can't go to jail," Hilary shouted.

Drew took another step toward her, but Hilary backed toward the cliff. She glanced over her shoulder, a strange look in her eyes. Jacob had seen that look before, the look of a criminal cornered and panicking. She was going to throw herself off the cliff.

"Hilary, please don't," Drew said, a calmness overcoming him. "Just think of our son. You don't want him to remember you like this."

She released a sob, her gun hand lowering, but inched backward.

Jacob raced forward and caught her just before she slipped over the edge.

He jerked the gun from her hand and tossed it into the dirt, then dragged her away from the cliff. She collapsed into a hysterical sobbing fit as Jacob snapped handcuffs around her wrists.

"Cora, it's all right," Jacob called. "You and Nina can come out now."

Hilary rocked herself back and forth, crying while Drew's gaze searched the woods.

A second later, Cora emerged from behind the boulder, carrying the little girl who was crying in her arms.

Brakes squealed, and the sound of an engine cut through the night. Liam. He was going into the house.

Cora looked at him with shock in her eyes.

"It's over," Jacob murmured. He wanted to go to her, but he had to guard Hilary.

Drew walked toward them, anguish, regret and awe on his face as Nina lifted her head.

"You didn't give up, you found her," Drew said in a raw whisper.

Cora nodded, although tears streamed down her face.

"I'm so sorry," Drew said. "I…didn't know. I swear I didn't."

Emotions colored Cora's face, but when Drew held out his arms, she and Nina went into them.

Jacob's heart squeezed. He had fulfilled his promise of reuniting Cora with her daughter.

Drew was the little girl's father, though. He'd also essentially admitted that he still loved Cora. It was obvious he was hurting.

The little girl deserved to have both of her parents together.

If that was what Cora wanted.

He had to give her time. They also had to deal with Faye. Cora didn't need pressure from him.

She needed to be with her little girl and make up for the years they'd missed.

Cora was so happy that Nina was safe she could barely contain her emotions. Yet Faye was Nina's mother. She pulled away from Drew and motioned to Jacob, mouthing that Faye was in the house.

A second later, Liam bolted through the woods. Jacob yelled out their location. Liam's gun was drawn, but he lowered it when he saw Jacob had handcuffed Hilary.

"Faye?" Cora mouthed to Liam.

He shook his head, his expression grave, and fresh tears blurred Cora's vision. She wanted Alice back, but she hadn't wanted Faye to die.

Nina would be brokenhearted. Faye was the only mother she'd ever known.

"I'm so sorry, Cora, so sorry," Drew murmured. He looked at Nina with such longing that Cora couldn't help but find forgiveness in her heart.

Cora choked back a sob. Nina—Alice—was going to need all the love she could get.

The next few minutes passed in a blur. An ambulance arrived, and Liam oversaw a crime scene team as they collected Hilary's gun and went in the house to process it.

The ME arrived and the ambulance loaded Faye's body to transport to the morgue.

Cora rocked her daughter in her arms while she waited. The little girl was so exhausted she fell asleep on Cora's shoulder.

"We'll run DNA to verify that she is Alice," Jacob told her.

"I'll start the paperwork to make sure that Cora is deemed the legal guardian." Drew stroked Cora's arm. "You won't ever be without your daughter again."

Emotions choked Cora as she hugged Nina to her.

Drew looked lost, then he gestured to Cora's car. "Sheriff, I'll drive her home. I know you have to transport Hilary to jail."

Jacob's mouth tightened, but he agreed.

Hilary screamed Drew's name, but he glared at her,

then turned his back on her, took Cora's arm and walked her and Nina to the car.

Cora looked back at Jacob, but he was all business. She hugged Nina to her, her heart soaring with happiness that she'd finally found Alice. The transition would be difficult for her baby, but she'd share the cards and presents and her letters, and help her daughter any way she needed.

Only now she had Alice back, did Jacob plan to walk out of her life?

Chapter Twenty-Seven

Six weeks later

Jacob had stayed away from Cora to give her and Alice time to adjust and get acquainted. But he missed Cora so much he hadn't slept in weeks. He dreamed of her. He fantasized about her. Hell, he'd even bought a damn ring.

A ring, for God's sake, when for all he knew, she might be deep in bed with her former husband, building back the family she'd lost.

He drove to her house anyway. He had to see for himself. He'd made up his mind he'd accept whatever she wanted, but his brothers had cornered him the night before during their weekly burger-and-beer night and told him he was a coward if he didn't tell her how he felt.

They were right. He was a coward.

No. Correction. He *had* been a coward. Now he was on his way to her house to confess his feelings like a lovestruck fool.

Unless she opened the door with Drew on her arm. Then he'd do what?

Fill them in on the case against Hilary. Tell her they'd arrested the man who'd shot at her, an ex-con Hilary had picked from one of Drew's former client lists. Liam had also busted the child kidnapping ring and made several arrests.

Then he'd act like he wasn't brokenhearted if she chose her damn ex over him.

Son of a bitch. Drew didn't deserve her.

He swung his car into her drive, the twinkling stars above glittering like the diamond in his pocket. He stuffed his hand inside and ran his finger over the velvet box. He hoped she liked it.

Hell, he hoped she wanted it. And him.

Cora's red SUV sat in the drive. He'd made sure her car was repaired and had it dropped off to her.

Drew's Mercedes was not in the drive.

A good sign.

He inhaled a deep breath, climbed out and walked up to her house. The door opened before he knocked. Cora stood on the other side, looking beautiful in a T-shirt and denim shorts, her long hair draped over one shoulder.

He ached to run his fingers through the silky strands.

"Jacob?"

"Yeah." *Nice opening, idiot.*

She shifted from foot to foot, her fingers curled around the doorjamb.

"Is Drew here?" he blurted.

Her brows bunched together in a frown. "No, why? Are you looking for him? Did Hilary get out of jail?"

He shook his head. "No, I just thought that Drew might be here. That the two of you, well, now that you have your little girl back, that you might…um…"

She made a low sound in her throat. "That we might what?"

"Reconcile," he said, deciding to confront the issue.

She crossed her arms. "No, Jacob. We didn't get back together just for Nina. But we have agreed that he'll be part of her life. He really didn't know what Hilary did."

"I understand." He started to back away, but she cleared her throat.

"Wait a minute. Why are you leaving?"

He silently called himself all kinds of names. He was acting like a moron. A coward. A cowardly moron.

His brothers had encouraged him to go for it. He had to tell her how he felt.

"I didn't want to interfere," Jacob said, his voice breaking.

"You aren't," she said. "Drew and I don't belong together, Jacob."

His heart skipped a beat. "You don't?"

Her lips curved into a smile. "No. How could I be with him when my heart belongs to someone else?"

Hope fluttered in his belly. He felt like he was an awkward fifteen-year-old.

He gave her a flirtatious look. "And who does it belong to?"

She leaned toward him, then pressed her hand against his cheek. "You."

Pure joy filled his chest. She angled her head to kiss him just as he dropped to one knee. He caught her before she pitched forward, and they both tumbled to the front porch.

Laughter spilled through the air, then he removed the ring from his pocket. "I messed this up, the proposal, but I love you, Cora, and I want to be with you."

Emotions glittered in her eyes. "I want to be with you, too. But you know I'm a package deal. We're still adjusting, but Nina has good days and bad ones. She'll stay in therapy as long as she needs to."

"I'm sure your love will help her heal."

"Like she's helping me. We've been working on my children's story. I'm planning to publish it soon."

"I'm so proud of you." Jacob's heart swelled with love and longing. He opened the ring box and held it out to her. "And I'm a patient man, Cora. I've been in love with you for years. We'll give Nina whatever she needs."

"Just love," Cora whispered. "That's all we both need."

He pulled her to him for a kiss. "I have plenty of that for both of you."

Then he slid the ring on her finger and closed his mouth over hers.

* * * * *

Look for the next book in
USA TODAY *bestselling author*
Rita Herron's Badge of Honor miniseries,
Left to Die,
available next month
from Harlequin Intrigue!

**WE HOPE YOU ENJOYED
THIS BOOK FROM**

⟨H⟩HARLEQUIN

INTRIGUE

Seek thrills. Solve crimes. Justice served.

Dive into action-packed stories that will keep you
on the edge of your seat. Solve the crime
and deliver justice at all costs.

6 NEW BOOKS AVAILABLE EVERY MONTH!

#1917 48 HOUR LOCKDOWN
Tactical Crime Division • by Carla Cassidy

When TCD special agent and hostage negotiator Evan Duran learns his ex, Annalise Taylor, and her students are being held hostage, he immediately rushes to the scene. They'll need to work together in order to keep everyone safe, but can they resolve the situation before it escalates further?

#1918 LEFT TO DIE
A Badge of Honor Mystery • by Rita Herron

When Jane Doe finds herself stranded in a shelter during a blizzard, all she knows is that she has suffered a head injury and ranger Fletch Maverick saved her. Can they discover the truth about Jane's past before an unseen enemy returns to finish what he started?

#1919 WHAT SHE DID
Rushing Creek Crime Spree • by Barb Han

Someone is terrorizing Chelsea McGregor and her daughter, and Texas rancher Nate Kent is the only person who can help Chelsea figure out who is after her. But can she trust an outsider to keep her family safe?

#1920 COVERT COMPLICATION
A Badlands Cops Novel • by Nicole Helm

Nina Oaks tried to forget Agent Cody Wyatt, but her old feelings come flooding back the moment she sees his face again. Now she's in danger—and so is Cody's daughter. He'll do anything to protect them both, even if that means confronting the most dangerous men in the Badlands.

#1921 HOSTILE PURSUIT
A Hard Core Justice Thriller • by Juno Rushdan

In twenty-four hours, marshal Nick McKenna's informant, Lori Carpenter, will testify against a powerful drug cartel. Nick has kept her safe for an entire year, but now, with a team of cold-blooded assassins closing in, he'll have to put it all on the line for his irresistible witness.

#1922 TARGET ON HER BACK
by Julie Miller

After discovering her boss has been murdered, Professor Gigi Brennan becomes the killer's next target. Her best chance at survival is Detective Hudson Kramer. Together, can they figure out who's terrorizing her...before their dreams of a shared future are over before they've even begun?

SPECIAL EXCERPT FROM

◆HARLEQUIN

INTRIGUE

The Tactical Crime Division—TCD—is a
specialized unit of the FBI.
They handle the toughest cases in remote locations.
A school invasion turned lockdown becomes personal
for hostage negotiator agent Evan Duran in
48 Hour Lockdown
by New York Times *bestselling author Carla Cassidy.*

Annalise's heart beat so fast her stomach churned with
nausea and an icy chill filled her veins. Bert was dead?
The security guard with the great smile who loved to tell
silly jokes was gone? And what two women had been
killed? Who had been in the office at the time of this…
this attack?

What were these killers doing here? What did they
want?

The sound of distant sirens pierced the air. The big
man cursed loudly.

"We were supposed to get in and out of here before
the cops showed up," the tall, thin man said with barely
suppressed desperation in his voice.

"Too late for that now," the big man replied. He
turned and pointed his gun at Annalise. She stiffened.
Was he going to kill her, as well? Was he going to shoot

her right now? Kill the girls? She put her arms around her students and tried to pull them all behind her.

More sirens whirred and whooped, coming closer and closer.

"Don't move," he snarled at them. He took the butt of his gun and busted out one of the windows. The sound of the shattering glass followed by a rapid burst of gunfire out the window made her realize just how dangerous this situation was.

The police were outside. She and her students were inside with murderous gunmen, and she couldn't imagine how this all was going to end.

Don't miss
48 Hour Lockdown by Carla Cassidy,
available March 2020 wherever
Harlequin Intrigue books and ebooks are sold.

Harlequin.com

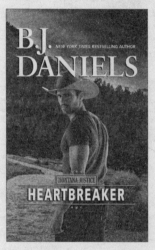

Chapter One

Her eyes flew open, her fight-or-flight response already
wide-awake. She jerked up in the bed, blinking wildly,
terrified and yet unable to believe what she was seeing.
Three hulking dark forms appeared out of the shadows of
the huge master bedroom. One of the men tripped over her
duffel bag on the floor where she'd dropped it. He swore as
he kicked it out of the way.

She tried hopelessly to banish the men back into whatever
nightmare they'd climbed out of, realizing the stumble must
have been what had awakened her.

All she could think rationally was that this couldn't be
happening, because these men being here tonight was so
wrong.

But before she could open her mouth to speak—let alone
scream—the largest of the three intruders reached her side
of the king-size bed. Roughly he pushed her down and
clamped a gloved hand over her mouth. This was real.

She finally screamed, but the gloved hand over her mouth muffled the sound. Not that it would have done any good if she had hollered to bloody hell. There was no one else in the house to come to her rescue—let alone anyone nearby. The house was high on the mountainside overlooking Flathead Lake, surrounded by acres of forest and as isolated as money could buy.

Frantically she shook her head as she met the man's eyes, the only feature not hidden by his black ski mask, and tried to communicate with him that she wasn't the woman he wanted.

"Don't fight me," the man said in a hoarse whisper as he renewed his efforts to hold her down. "We don't want to hurt you."

But she did fight because they were making a terrible mistake and they didn't know it. That realization sent panic rocketing through her system. Her heart banged against her rib cage, her thundering pulse deafening in her ears. She fought to pull the clamp from her mouth.

If she could only explain the error they were making. Failing in her attempts to pull away his gloved hand, she struck out with her fists as her legs kicked wildly to free themselves from the covers. All she'd managed to do was to make things worse. He leaned over her, pressing his body weight against her chest with his forearm, taking away her breath.

"Did you find it?"

Don't miss
Heartbreaker by B.J. Daniels,
available April 2020 wherever
HQN books and ebooks are sold.

HQNBooks.com